THE GALLERIES SERIES
BOOK 1

I0574046

# *the* art *of* seeing truth

## A SPLASH OF ART
## & MYSTERY

# JAN MURPHY

Published by Sweet Pea Press
Design and distribution by Bublish

ISBN: 978-1-64704-789-4 (paperback)
ISBN: 978-1-64704-780-1 (ebook)

*To Sweet Pea*

Art is the lie that enables us to realize the truth.
—Pablo Picasso

# ONE

Artists notice things. The palest orange on the prickly center of a dahlia. Inky purple resting on mountaintops, exhausted after a storm.

Nina ached to paint it all.

Serious artists thought that way. Every eyeful either sparked a desire to paint or brought to mind a finished painting.

Nina glanced at the wall sconces in the Caspian Hotel hallway and thought of one of her favorites: a monarch butterfly. The prism of jewel tones above the sconces created a distinct fan pattern similar to her butterfly watercolor. She recalled the praise she had received from colleagues over her technique. She sat with that a moment before continuing along the hall.

The Aspen County Art Society held an annual contest. This year, she had received the nod to judge. It wasn't surprising. She'd worked hard, getting her name out there and entering her paintings in prestigious nationwide shows. The Caspian, mere steps from The Art Loft where Nina worked, made judging convenient. She wouldn't have to juggle her part-time shifts.

She adored her job. Spouting facts about artists no better than herself to lookie-loo tourists punching their annual culture card kept her focused. Tisha (the name her mother preferred instead of Patricia) lived close by The Galleries, an urban oasis of kitschy art shops and creative alcoves that covered a swath of land behind the Caspian. Backlit by blue-green, jagged mountains, The Galleries spread out like a labyrinth surrounded by evergreens, The Art Loft nestled inside. Occasional lunches with Tisha always proved amusing. The twosome was yin and yang; Tisha, mischievous and forthright; Nina, serious minded.

The Caspian's vibe, with bear rugs, timber-lined walls, and oversize hearths, reminded Nina of a mountain retreat as she continued along the hallway. A cozy couple approached Nina. She tucked her practical, low-heeled shoes against the wall and found a tired smile. After hours of scrutinizing lifeless artwork, drab colors, and paint-by-number canvases at best, she craved a sudsy bath. She held the painful smile as the pair walked by. Perhaps their children were with in-laws while they enjoyed a weekend getaway exploring galleries or venturing up to Pikes Peak on the cog railway before winter blanketed Colorado.

None of that interested Nina. She wasn't at the Caspian to enjoy herself. No, judging an art contest gave her credibility. Always focused on her end goal, she had gritted her teeth through the two-day judging stint. Mentally, she clicked judging off her list, which was more of a game plan really, leading to her own art exhibit. And eventually, her art hanging in someone's living room, purchased at a hefty price.

The couple ducked down another hallway. Nina sighed. *A bath and a single malt.* Glenlivet sounded perfect. Her go-to whiskey. Maybe she would order room service. Soak until she pruned.

Her phone chimed. She plucked the cell from her purse and opened the text message.

*Congratulations, Nina! The Artist Network has recognized your high skill level in watercolor. You have been awarded Best of Show, top honors at this year's showcase competition. More to follow via email. Just wanted to share the great news! Carol, Director of Awards.*

Nina nearly dropped the phone. She never giggled. Yet she did, then looked around to see if anyone had noticed. Quickly tugging at the hemmed edges of her suit jacket, she tried to gather herself. The judging committee expected that Nina. But she couldn't. Wouldn't, at least in this moment, act all together and professional. She'd waited years for this and felt drunk on the words. She needed another read. Another fix. Or maybe she didn't believe it.

She glanced at the screen again. The words hadn't changed: *Best of Show. Top honors. Wow.* Grinning widely, she looked away. Pride lightened her heart. Floating this high brought an unexpected tingling to every nerve ending.

The bath could wait. She needed a drink.

For an average-looking forty-four-year-old with a blunt, sharp-angled, chestnut bob to go with her structured life, she didn't look like a whiskey drinker. More of a girl-next-door type who dabbled in rosé and listened and nodded until conversations faded. Her quiet confidence fooled most folks. While she did listen and nod—say, at a party—she would also scope out her surroundings. Something always caught her eye. A vase. A delicate woven fabric. A glint of light dappling a table. All delicious morsels to memorize and add to a painting later.

"Yoo-hoo!"

Nina turned. Another judge from the art contest paraded up to her. *What was her name?* The silver-haired woman wore a loose braid roped over her shoulder that wiggled against her chest like a slippery fish out of water.

"Did I miss much?" Nina had skipped the meeting after the competition. She'd done her part. Still, a twinge of guilt surfaced.

"Not really." The woman shrugged. "Standard stuff. No fraternizing with the art contestants afterward. Keeping things professional."

*Congratulations . . . Best of Show.*

Nina blinked, focused back on the woman. "Rules," Nina said offhandedly. She liked rules. Follow them, and you were usually rewarded or at least pleased that you stayed the course.

They continued along the hallway. "Did you see the blurb?" The woman fished a folded paper from her pocket and opened it. "Here." She angled the paper toward Nina. "The contest made page nine of the *Pikes Peak Bulletin*. Cool doggies." She read a few lines.

Nina neither bothered to look nor offer a response. Was one expected? She wasn't good at reading those types of interactions. At the corridor, a sign affixed to the wall pointed left toward guest rooms. She paused and fingered the key card in her pocket. She couldn't go to her room. She needed whiskey. At least one shot. "I need a drink," she said in a whisper, not realizing the words had seeped out.

"I'll join you," the woman chimed in.

Looking pleased with herself, Nina read the kind slant of the woman's eyes tracking hers. *She thinks she's made a friend.* Nina didn't do friends. She hid her indifference and smiled.

The woman patted the left side of her chest, below her exposed bra strap. She frowned. "My cash is in my room. Give me a sec."

Nina wanted solitude. A quiet booth in the bar where she could toast herself and relish the achievement she'd longed for. Was that too much to ask?

Reluctantly, she nodded and watched the woman stride down the hallway before following the sign pointing toward the bar. The decorative sconces she had admired earlier flickered. Nina glanced up, and her mother's voice came to mind. *An imbalance in light. It's a sign,* she would say. Nina considered it all bunk. Still, she had an odd feeling. Nothing she could even describe. She shrugged and continued to the bar. What harm could there be in a celebratory drink? Nina strolled inside and settled on a barstool.

A sad-looking man slouched at the far end of the counter. Broad-shouldered, he wore a childish, red cap of some sort pulled down over his ears, making him look ridiculous. Besides Nina, he was the only other patron at the bar. Nina would have ignored him, but he kept tapping his stubby fingers on the shiny bar top, annoying her.

The bartender glanced over.

"Glenlivet on the rocks, water back." She offered a polite smile.

He slid a tumbler toward her and rattled the ice in the glass. By her standards, the whiskey pour was short. Still, she liked the sound of ice swimming in the smoky liquid. She took a sip and closed her eyes, the spirit burning in a good way.

She shifted toward the hallway. No sign of Ms. Silver Hair. Nina's foot bounced on the rung of the stool. She was still high from the news. Too high. Jittery. Another slow sip.

The sad man's chair scraped against the tile floor. She glanced at him and caught movement near another hallway adjacent to the bar. A quick hand reached across the carpet, nabbing something. Their eyes met briefly. A girl. A brief burst of brown hair before she disappeared into the inky shadows of the hall.

Nina shrugged, plucked a twenty from her shoulder bag. She wasn't waiting for Ms. Silver Hair. She downed the whiskey and asked for another. Fresh drink in hand, she slid the cash on the counter and drifted past the sad man now tapping his empty glass. Another swig of the whiskey.

She moseyed along that hallway behind the bar where she'd seen the girl. Less of a chance of running into Ms. Silver Hair, she figured. Eventually, Nina would land somewhere. She was in no hurry. This award, this moment, deserved fanfare.

And whiskey.

Guest rooms lined the quiet hall. An ice machine churned. Nina jumped, almost losing an ice cube. She steadied her glass and continued walking. Just past a stairwell, a child stood outside a room, two fingers filling her mouth. Was it the same girl? She had the same unkempt hair.

On seeing Nina, the girl's almond-shaped, brown eyes widened. Nina opened her mouth to say something. Hello? Wasn't that what you said to a child? Instead, Nina pasted on an awkward smile. The little brat shoved out her bottom lip before slipping inside the room and shutting the door.

Nina shrugged. No one was going to ruin her celebration. Lifting the tumbler, she drained the glass. A phone rang mid-gulp, the shrillness hurting her ears.

Across the hall, a guest room door stood open. Inside, an older man with sandy hair was slumped in a bucket chair. Nina inched closer, just outside his door.

A shaft of light leaked in through the curtains, like a pointer across the carpet landing on the man's legs, which were turned outward. He appeared uncomfortable. A limp arm hung over the edge of the chair.

*He's asleep,* she concluded, and stepped past the door. The annoying phone boomed again.

Something, she realized, bothered her. She leaned back, grasped the edge of the door, and peeked inside.

Another series of rings. Nina jumped. The man, however, didn't move a leg, an arm. Anything.

"Excuse me," Nina said, hoping he would wake up. Louder this time, she said, "Are you all right, sir?"

More incessant ringing.

"Damn," she mumbled and crept inside the room.

Still holding the glass, she inched closer. Rounding the chair, she gasped.

Half-slit eyes stared through her. Blue-tinged lips formed a perfect O as if the poor man wanted to say something.

*Holy shit.*

Nina slugged back the glass, opened wide to receive what she desperately needed. Only ice.

Fingers shaking, she reached out toward the body, but quickly snapped back, her hand forming a fist at her side.

Paramedics barreled in. Nina glanced up, dazed, as a burly man wearing an orange vest pushed past her.

"Out in the hall, ma'am." The clipped words came with brief eye contact before he knelt to one knee in front of the ashen figure. "What happened?"

Nina's free arm hugged her stomach. "I . . . I don't know." She pointed to the door with the hand holding the glass. "I was just . . ." She couldn't think.

The paramedic checked the stubbled slope of the man's neck for a pulse. While he placed a device on the man's middle finger, another paramedic rattled in carrying a compact case. He camped beside the chair. Snap, snap. The case unfolded. Nina scanned the wonder drugs and licked her lips, hopeful.

"What's wrong? Is he . . .?" Her eyes narrowed on the lifeless figure and then turned back to the duo at his side.

The oddest thought came to her: *Recite a chant*. Ridiculous, she knew, but it had worked when Aunt Sissy, age eighty-four, had decided to stand on a ladder to change a chandelier bulb and toppled over. Nina's mother had babbled something about white gold. *Feel the healing energy, visualize bright light.* At the time, Nina had rolled her eyes as her mother had drawn wide circles in the air above Aunt Sissy's damaged legs positioned like a bent paper clip on the ceramic tile. Nina considered it hooey, yet here she was, willing the man in the chair to wake up.

"Bright light," she whispered. "Bright light."

Much like a well-rehearsed play, the younger, clean-shaven paramedic lowered his ear to the man's nose. His hand dropped to the man's wrist, checking for a pulse.

*Take a breath. Come on. Breathe.* "Bright light."

With less care than a living body should be afforded, the paramedics lifted the man off the chair and onto the carpet. CPR began. Scissors ripped across the pinstriped shirt. Paper-thin patches were pressed against his still, lily-white chest.

A part of her was fascinated by the calm orchestration among the paramedics. Minimal words. Subtle gestures. The unconscious man well cared for. Nina bit her lip. Without awareness, a part of her past slipped into the room, like a familiar odor she had thought she had forgotten.

Sensing someone in her periphery, Nina glanced out the door. The same girl from across the hall leaned against a woman. Her mother, Nina assumed, because they shared the same almond-shaped eyes and bark-brown hair parted down the middle. Seeing Nina's probing stare, the mother looped an arm across the child's chest like protective armor.

The machine attached to the electrodes beeped. Nina shifted her eyes back, steadied her gaze on the flat line on the screen, willing it to rise. After all her years of preferring the black and white of things, her mother's quirky dead-people-speak-to-me nonsense had somehow become real. Or at least held possibility. And her father's utmost decorum that Nina had always followed flew out the hotel window.

The odor returned, robbing her breath. And a familiar vision flashed behind her eyes. She began to sweat and swiped the back of her hand across her brow. Suddenly, she couldn't breathe or see anything other than what had happened six months ago at her father's house. Her eyes widened, trailed down to the man on the floor. *How could the same thing be happening?* She swallowed. The bite of whiskey had left her tongue thick and dry.

The beeping stopped. The crease in the man's navy trousers lay freshly pressed. Fitting suit pants for any occasion. The rest of him looked like a crash cart at the ER. Barefoot, his plump toes were lily white, like his chest. With all the wires and patches, Nina hadn't given up hope. Surely something could revive him.

The case, filled with syringes, tubes, and bandages, snapped shut. The sound echoed within the quiet four walls. The clean-shaven paramedic lowered his chin to the mic fastened to his collar and rattled off code numbers. She didn't need to understand. She knew.

"The police are on their way." He offered Nina a faint, practiced smile that was handed out in these situations. "Don't leave," he warned.

For the second time, he motioned her out to the hall. This time, she obeyed.

She should never have entered the room.

# TWO

**W**ithout as much as a glance, the lanky police officer swaggered past Nina in the hallway and entered the hotel room. The mother, clutching her daughter, stood across the hall. Nina managed a smile, though she sensed judgment in the woman's narrowed eyes.

A pencil-thin maid passed by pushing a squeaky cart. Nina reached out and tucked her glass in between the tiny bottles of shampoo. As if this had happened before, the woman met Nina's eyes and lifted one side of her mouth before pushing the cart along.

Nina's fingers were cold and stiff from strangling the ice-filled glass. She was rubbing them when the police officer stepped out.

"Detective Kanoy." He pointed to his shiny badge. "Can you tell me why you were in Mr. Wood's room?" He was squinting. She couldn't decide if this was his interrogation face or if his left eye simply wouldn't open.

*Mr. Wood.* The name sounded familiar. On second thought, maybe not. Nina shook her head. "I was looking for a place to sit. Somewhere," she added, "besides the bar."

One eyebrow rose. He examined the length of her, a long look that ended with a smirk. "How much have you had to drink today?"

She wanted to rip that smirk off his face. "What does that matter?" Nina pulled away from the wall, straightened up, and tried her best to gather her thoughts. "I saw the man." She motioned a hand toward the room as if that somehow explained everything. "He appeared to be in distress." A quick dip of her gaze onto the scribble on his notepad and he shifted the pad closer to his starched blues.

"So he was alive when you entered the room?"

"No." She rubbed her temple. "I . . . I don't know."

Kanoy shot a glance over his shoulder. "The girl says she saw you walk into the room and stand over the body."

Nina glowered at the girl, who promptly slipped her head into the folds of her mother's jacket. Nina shook her head before her eyes slanted back to the officer. "I was walking by," she explained. "That's all." She paused, then recounted, "The phone rang. When he didn't move, I entered to see if he was okay." Satisfied with her response, she glared back at him.

"Did you attempt CPR?"

"Well . . . no."

*Last time.*

She blinked away the image of her father lying on the floor, his eyes glassy and fixed, head tilted to the side where she kneeled, holding his limp hand, squeezing his fingers, begging him to come to.

"Did you check his pulse?"

She looked down, offered a barely audible, "No."

"Why didn't you call 911, ma'am?"

*Because last time . . .*

"Did you know the man?" Kanoy bellowed when she didn't answer his question. Cool-gray eyes burrowed into her, waiting. Impatiently, he shifted his stance.

Nina rubbed her forehead. "I don't know," she simply said and tossed up her hands.

"The hotel shows him registered here for an art contest." He held out a business card. In foil letters, below his name, Sam Wood's achievements shimmered. All the accolades she'd dreamed of. Without thought, she took the card from Kanoy's hand and slid a thumb over the words, like reading braille. *Master Artist Designation.* Her tongue skated across her lips.

Realizing she had sidetracked, she bent forward, focused on the name on the card. "Yes," she said, nodding. "Wood. I faintly remember the name." From where, she didn't recall.

"We spoke with his wife, Odilia. He came to the Springs to see the artist he'd handpicked. Her name is Nina . . ."

". . . Shubert." They said the last name in unison.

Nina smoothed her shoulder-length bob, perfect as the morning's blow dry. Whether on purpose or not, she stood taller and cleared her throat. "I'm Nina Shubert."

He looked at her critically, a sneer tugging at his lips. "You must admit it looks peculiar you here in Mr. Wood's room."

# THREE

The following morning, standing four deep in the hotel checkout line, Nina lifted her head to the cool air streaming down from a vent.

She couldn't wait to ditch the place. Next stop: home. She was trying, really trying to shake the image of Sam Wood in the chair. After the detective had turned her loose last night, she had retreated to her room and ordered a drink. That had helped. This morning, though, 9:00 a.m. was too early for whiskey.

She brushed a thread off her pleated, black pants. She couldn't help noticing the chatty woman behind the counter. Specifically, every time her thin, tangerine-stained lips formed an O, resembling the mouth of the dead man. But his mouth had remained slightly parted, as if he had tried to say something. The last something. The words, she was sure, were somewhere in the room, scattered like dust. Soon a house cleaner would wipe them away with a cloth, laden with lemony polish.

Nina had found her father much like Sam Wood in the chair. Cheeks hollowed, creped skin over a bony temple. A whiskered jaw. Nina forced away the image.

A whimper escaped from inside a pet carrier on the carpet in front of her. Nina glanced down at the fluff ball scratching at the cage. A kind-looking man with a shock of blue hair dropped to a knee and tried soothing the pup.

"I couldn't find you last night."

Nina turned.

Ms. Silver Hair. Nina had conveniently tried to forget her. Why couldn't she remember her name? She'd never been good at names. Or faces, for that matter.

Nina forced a smile. Thankfully, Ms. Silver Hair was still wearing the name tag from the art show underneath her jacket. *Mauve.* More a color than a name.

"Did you do anything fun last night?" Mauve's eyebrows rose.

Nothing about this weekend registered as fun. "I turned in early." Nina fished the room key from her pocket. "You?"

Mauve said something about finding a jazz trio outside the restaurant Pie-pie in The Galleries. A few of the judges had landed there last night. Nina nodded and inched forward when the man with the dog hefted the crate onto the counter, giving Tangerine Lips a startle.

Mauve snuck in behind Nina. She began telling the woman behind her the same tale. When the crated pooch and its owner were finished, Nina stepped up to the counter. "Nina Shubert, room sixteen to check out." She slid the room key on the counter.

"Nina?" a loud voice splintered from behind. "Nina Shubert?"

Nina turned.

A ruddy-cheeked woman emerged from the line. "You're the woman who judged my painting."

Nina gulped and prayed this had nothing to do with Sam Wood. "Have we met?" She flashed a brief smile.

The lady paraded forward and shoved a paper at Nina. It was a scorecard. "You gave me an overall score of two out of ten for my painting." The woman, fighting back tears, waited for a response.

Nina's mouth hung open. She had nothing. Her mind flashed to the paintings she'd judged. *Lilies Floating in Water.* The artist had tried too hard to copy Monet. *Mia,* a self-portrait, had offered zero color contrast. There had been one promising canvas, *Pears on Table.* Simple subject. Fair interpretation of light.

Nina glanced at the scorecard. *Fanny's Farm.* Yes. She remembered the piece and nodded. Primitive design. Repeated flat shapes.

Before her lips could form words, the woman yanked the scorecard away. Teary-eyed, she read from it. "A kindergartner could have produced a more interesting painting." She paused, sniffled. "Do you even know what folk art is?" Folding the card stock in half, she handed it back to Nina as if to say, "It's yours. I don't want it."

Solemnly, Nina took the card. She didn't know what to do. Everyone in the line was quaking. She swallowed. "Of course I know folk art." At least she thought she did.

Empathy wasn't her strong suit. Awkwardly, she reached out, touched the woman's shoulder. The woman ducked away from Nina's outstretched arm. She'd never been good with people. Only paintbrushes.

"Nine months I worked on that canvas. A tad of encouragement. Is that too much to ask?"

"Scores are part of the process." Immediately, Nina brought a hand to her mouth, wishing she could stuff the words back inside. Clearly, it had been the wrong thing to say. And everyone was watching, waiting. Including Ms. Silver Hair—um, Mauve. Lost on what was expected of her, Nina reached inside her purse, then pulled a tissue from a packet tucked away for such occasions. But she wasn't a crier. Only once had tears flowed. The day she had found her father in a chair.

Nina fidgeted with the tissue. She wanted to dash for the door but found herself caught up in the grief she'd inflicted on this woman, with what had happened to Sam Wood, and as much as she'd tried over the last six months, the circumstances surrounding her father. It all swirled around her, vacuous, robbing her breath.

She licked her dry lips. She needed a drink.

The click of heels sounded. The large-breasted art director emerged from the crowd. She wore a frilly blouse and billowy skirt, no doubt to offset her large frame. *Now what?* Nina rallied with a brittle smile. "Hello, Joan." At least she remembered her name.

In the distance, behind Joan, Detective Kanoy leaned against the wall. Arms crossed, he nodded, wielding a knowing smile directly at Nina.

Nina dismissed him and focused on Joan. "You talked to him?"

Joan briefly glanced at Kanoy before turning back. "We've got a problem."

# FOUR

"Sorry, I have to go." Nina couldn't stomach another confrontation. She broke eye contact with Joan.

"You look upset." Joan bit her lower lip, searched out Nina's eyes.

Of course she was upset. What exactly had Kanoy told her? Maybe she was overreacting. Maybe Joan wanted to talk about the score she'd given *Fanny's Farm*? Nina had never thought to ask the painter her name. Was it Fanny? She looked like a Fanny.

Nina swallowed. Her gut told her otherwise. It was about lifeless Sam Wood. Bone and flesh only, an ashen shell of man whose life had ended on her watch. A quick glance over Joan's shoulder and Nina took a breath. Kanoy had disappeared. Still, nervous energy hammered in her chest. Could Joan hear the thump, thump?

The distant clatter of voices interrupted her thoughts. Joan, pursing her lips, was looking at Nina carefully, waiting for her to say something. Distracted, Nina's eyes traveled around the room, searching for Kanoy.

"We'll contact you when we sort this out." Joan smiled, crinkling her kind eyes. "We'll talk then."

Nina didn't care when. She had to get out of there. She managed a nod and zipped past Joan down a narrow corridor and pushed open a door with the brute force of her shoulder.

Outside, crisp, cold air filled her lungs. September brought brisk winds, and this year was no different. She buttoned her suit jacket. Leaves scattered across the sidewalk and took flight as she clumped along the back alley toward the street.

She glanced back at the hotel, a brick fortress rising into the clouds. Her stomach lurched. She couldn't get far enough away from the scene in the lobby. Or Kanoy. And the man in the chair kept appearing behind her eyes. Telling her something, but what?

A gate led off the hotel grounds into The Galleries. After what had happened, Nina needed a minute before heading to the parking garage. She strayed left and followed a cement path skirting the hub of popular shops, including The Art Loft. Running into coworkers wasn't an option. She needed time to sift through what had happened. She was built that way. Always shuffling through the what-ifs to the nth degree.

She passed a boho shop selling miscellaneous fair-trade merch. Tisha often dragged her inside, picked up several thingamajigs, and poked fun at Nina for being far too serious. Apparently, Nina hadn't gotten the playful gene. A part of her envied her mother for that reason. Nina tried to be fun, but her forced antics always fell flat.

She walked farther along the curved path. Thick ferns framed the next shop, a florist Nina had never used.

Behind her, footsteps clapped on the pavement.

She twisted, her pulse quickening. No one was there. Nina stepped inside the shop. Kanoy could be following her.

Inside, a thickset woman bent over a bucket, stripping thorns off roses. She wiped her wrinkled cheek with the back of a gloved hand. "May I help you?"

"I'd like to order flowers." She hadn't planned to, yet here she was.

"What's the occasion? What did you have in mind?"

Nina swiveled, admiring the prepared florals and plants arranged on ornate shelves. She wanted something specific. Something that said sorry for the low score. She didn't have to explain herself to this woman. She sidestepped, away from a direct view from passersby outside. "You choose," she said.

"Is this a delivery?"

"I'll take them with me."

While the woman gathered flowers, Nina walked the length of a glass refrigerated room flanking the wall. Inside, a man fussed with curly willow branches gathered in a bucket. Another bucket held basil-like leaves and walnut-shaped berries. He exited and rubbed his hands together. He offered Nina a quick glance before addressing the shop owner. "Did you pick up the order on the machine for Forest Greens? A delivery next Thursday."

The woman pulled off a generous length of ribbon from a spool. "Poor guy." She held the arrangement she'd prepared at arm's length, tilted her head, adjusted a stem or two before resting the bouquet on the butcher block.

"Died right here at the Caspian." The man looked directly at Nina, deep-set eyes hard and probing. "Could be murder." He nodded. "That's what they're saying."

The man continued to stare. Nina broke eye contact, shifted behind a greeting card stand. She snatched a random card, shimmied until she stood completely out of sight.

*Who was saying murder?*

The crinkle of cellophane wrapping. The snip of scissors. "Had a wife and two kids. What a shame, eh?" A long, reflective sigh followed.

Nina tucked the card back into the stand. Slowly, she crept backward toward the door. She eased the door open with her backside, careful not to make a sound, and slipped outside.

Cool air burned her throat. She hurried along the path. There was a pottery store hitched on a rise of stones meant to look like a weathered outpost on a hill. A narrow breezeway separated the pottery shop from the next store. Nina slipped between the buildings and slumped against the worn timber.

*I didn't murder anybody.*

That word, *murder,* made her feel dirty, different. The inference somehow penetrated deep. Sam Wood in the chair, his ghostly stare, parted lips. She couldn't wipe away what she saw. Not even when she closed her eyes.

She reached into her pocket. Phone in her palm, she stared at it. Whom could she call? She needed a calm, steady voice. Someone to say this wasn't happening.

Or a shot of whiskey would do.

She thumbed through her contacts, bypassing her mother. She would ask unsettling questions, leaving Nina to defend her actions.

She scrolled further. Mostly acquaintances, distant as second cousins. Long ago, she'd sworn off girlfriends. They were no different than her paintings, demanding too much attention and falling short of expectations. She hovered over Stacey's name, the owner of The Art Loft. The woman made a killer dirty martini and could spot a forged painting from twenty yards. But Stacey stuck to business. No personal stuff.

Desperation caught in Nina's throat. Her troubles were mounting. Now two men had fallen gravely ill in her presence. What were the chances?

The next name stole her breath.

He wouldn't answer, of course, but she could hear his recorded voice. Stately and far too serious. She got that in spades from him.

She tapped the number, closed her eyes, and listened to her father's voice.

# 1985

# FIVE

Samuel Wood had one warm memory from his childhood: Big Dream Bookstore. Every week during story time, he would stare out the window. Eventually, he'd wiggle from his mother's lap and gallop to the window, where the city park unfolded across the street. Hearing the stories from the window, where he could fidget and dance around, made the stories that much better.

He'd always resisted confinement. Even in college. Halfway through his second year, he had bolted. Six months later—today, to be exact—he found himself sitting in the bookstore parking lot staring at *Help Wanted* ads for jobs for which he wasn't remotely qualified. The bookstore was low-hanging fruit. Not anyone's dream job for sure. Certainly not his. Yet here he was on the outskirts of Colorado Springs, where he had lived his whole life. Residents of the Springs considered the city of Broadmoor the town on the other side of the tracks. It poached on the edge of Colorado Springs proper.

A week into the bookstore job, Sam slipped away from his duties. Someone had caught his attention.

"Books await, Sam." Martha, the owner, pushed her stylish glasses up her pointed nose and settled into her sturdy hands-on-hips pose.

Sam sighed, retreated from watching the blonde reading to a semicircle of rambunctious toddlers. It was just as well. The UPS driver had knocked at the back door, followed by the vroom of an overworked engine. The tight kitchen doubled as a back room where gently used books were stacked precariously and the staff gulped down coffee and nibbled Martha's pastry du jour. Today: chocolate-filled croissants. Sam snuck a flaky bite and brushed a hand on his jeans before wedging the door open with a sneaker and hefting two boxes off the back porch.

It was his day to examine the drop-offs for dog-eared pages and cracked spines. Martha handled the new books from the UPS delivery. She would sashay from room to room, arranging the new books just so, like baubles on display. Under the stairs, Martha had fashioned a nook with pillows and a manger of stuffed animals. As a child, Sam had played with other kids there. According to his mother, a time or two, he had fallen asleep cradling a book. Another warm memory.

Lingering memories about the nook had stuck with him. Maybe he remembered being an ordinary kid there. Playing with others and away from his father, safe among the books. Sam's father got noticed because of his remarkable face. Not in a good way. Bushy brows. Gray, piercing eyes always finding something wrong. Never without a ChapStick, he would smooth it over his cracked lips that couldn't seem to smile. In the nook, Sam wasn't Edward Wood III's kid. Just Sam.

Sam wasn't in the mood to sort books. He poked his head into the parlor where Skylar, the slim girl with flippy blonde hair, continued to read to the children.

". . . Now he wasn't hungry anymore, and he wasn't a little caterpillar anymore."

The light from the window struck her eyes. She squinted, adjusting her lanky limbs in the oversize chair. Barring clouds, light flooded that wedge of the carpet midway through the afternoon reading. With the grace of a gazelle, she slid onto the carpet, folded those never-ending legs beneath her, and delivered the next line without a hitch. A crooked smile broke across Sam's face, deepening his dimples.

Martha appeared in the doorway. "Did we get the delivery, Sam?"

He pointed at the brown boxes stacked beside the fridge. "Only two this week."

Her glance fell to the table overrun with books. "You've got work to do."

He plucked a book from the table. All for show, of course. As soon as she disappeared around the corner, he ditched the hardback and fingered another flaky bite of his pastry.

He didn't care for Martha. The woman flaunted her wealth. Designer clothes and god-awful jewelry like the coral brooch pinned to her prim silk blouse today. He loathed her rigid posture. Old money demanded sweeping glances, conveying superiority.

He had a knack for recognizing the upper crust; he'd been raised on it, chewed it up, and spat it out. As a tyke, he had become a bothersome chore best left to the help, followed by years at boarding school. On holidays, his parents had sent for him. They hadn't wanted him. He could see it in his father's dull and distracted eyes. No in-between with his father. His eyes either hazed over with disinterest or flared bright with rage. Sam wasn't enough. As a boy, he hadn't understood. Now the differences glared in his face. And his own disappointment in his father had turned to anger. Like his father, Sam's eyes were gray, a lighter shade, pleasing and bright. The two men shared a square jaw and waves of golden-brown hair. Yet they looked nothing alike; his father's appearance demanded attention, like a spirited stallion, while Sam drifted by unnoticed.

Sam lacked Edward's kill-or-be-killed attitude. Maybe nice guys did finish last, but he would take that any day. And he did. After dropping out of college, with only a backpack and a couple hundred bucks in his pocket, he had settled into a modest trailer park under a clump of blue pines on the banks of the Taylor River. Running water and a toilet. Canned tuna and a beer most nights. Maybe grilled cheese. It was all he needed.

Now, after sorting two stacks of books, Sam gathered the keepers and started tucking mysteries on shelves when Skylar waltzed up.

"Do we have *Matilda*? Didn't see it on the PC." Martha had bought the latest tech craze—an IBM personal computer.

"I saw a couple of titles by Dahl." Sam shrugged. "Not sure about that one." He scanned the author's name on the book he held and tucked it on a shelf. "How'd you like reading to the kids?"

"Beats shelving books." She winked and pulled the length of her hair to one side. A slow smile filled her face, like a sunrise breaking the horizon. Sam waited it out until she caught him staring. He plucked another book from the cart and pretended to be interested in the cover.

"Off to find *Matilda*," Skylar said over her shoulder.

"Hey, you up for coffee after work?" He couldn't believe that had fallen from his lips. The thump in his chest double-timed, waited.

Sam didn't date much. It came down to money, really. He didn't have any and girls expected it. To say he hated everything about money was an understatement. But he did enjoy a girl's company. Some girls even liked the clumsy, low-self-confidence type. And luckily, those were the girls he generally attracted.

"We could talk shop." *That sounded lame.* He ducked, adjusted a book, and eyeballed her through the bookshelf.

He liked Skylar. Dressed in T-shirts and jeans most days, she didn't pretend to be anyone special. And there was beauty in that, making her special after all. Playful freckles danced across her button nose. She had a quiet presence that drew him in.

Sam could hear Skylar clicking the pen in her hand. Feeling entirely silly, he rose.

"Sure." She shrugged. "Coffee sounds nice."

Donovan's served a killer pecan pie. Sam remembered the place from spring-break vacations. For a five-spot, he could splurge on dessert and coffee.

He chose the outside patio. A cool breeze rippled through the aspens, and most folks had opted for inside seating. Sam sat at a table visible from the street and waited.

Skylar sauntered up wearing a loose-fitting dress, cinched tight at the waist with a belt-like contraption. He glanced down at the faded Mötley Crüe T-shirt and jeans he'd worn to work. Strike one.

"You changed." He smiled and hoped to God she couldn't tell he was nervous. But he was always nervous and fidgety. Impulsive too. That's what usually got him in trouble.

"I have a thing later." She shrugged and slid into the seat across the table.

The waiter appeared, and they ordered coffee. He managed to pull off small talk. Did she like her schedule? Would she read in the afternoons more often?

"I guess we're talking shop," she said after their coffees arrived. Her fingertip lazily circled the rim of the mug.

"I guess I stink at this." Sam wiped his brow.

"No. Work's all we know about each other." She leaned in. "Tell me something I don't know about you, Sam Wood." She pinned him with bright eyes.

Sam wriggled uncomfortably in the wrought iron chair. "From zero to a hundred. You don't mess around." This side of her—animated, bold—surprised him. He wasn't sure he liked it.

"I'll start then." She settled back, glanced beyond him. A thought came to her, and her lips widened. "I help Martha with a side business," she announced with a punch of pride.

"Doing what?"

"Special book orders." She blew on the coffee. "Every so often, I deliver books after work."

"You drop off books to kids?" He frowned. "Why can't they come to the bookstore?"

"Not kids." She made a face. "Adult collectors."

Sam jiggled the idea in his head. "With the pay Martha offers, it hardly seems worth the effort. Besides, what do they do with the books?"

"I guess what most people do: put them on a shelf somewhere." She shrugged. "Like prized possessions."

"Collecting dust," Sam added. He didn't get it. They were just books.

While Skylar rattled off a list of customers, he fingered the twenty in his jeans pocket. All he had until payday. He drew a blank on the names she mentioned. Then again, he'd lived at boarding school most of his life. Anyway, the delivery business didn't particularly interest him.

"Earth to Sam."

"Sorry." He sat up taller in the chair. "My turn, I guess." He strummed his fingers on the plastic tablecloth. "Nothing comes to mind." He didn't have any dark secrets, hidden skills, or prized possessions worth mentioning. If anything, his father had drummed into him two simple facts: he wasn't anything special, and he'd never be successful.

When he didn't speak, Skylar's face soured. "Really?" She recoiled, disinterest clouding her eyes.

"Sorry. Pretty dull existence, huh?" He rubbed at his temple. "Maybe my time hasn't come. When I get a life, I'll let you know." He was joking. Sort of.

She shook her head. "I don't give up that easily." She considered him for a time. "Tell me something about you, Sam Wood. What do you really want?"

Maybe she expected him to say a new car, a techy gadget like a Walkman, or a better job. Honestly, he wanted none of that. He'd been living on anger at his father, at everything he represented. That was enough.

He studied Skylar across the table, backlit by puffy clouds eating up the sky. A flicker of something warmed his bones. For a moment, the hard edges of his anger softened. Maybe he imagined it, but he liked it. Really liked it. But he wondered, *If my anger subsides, then what?*

"So what is it, Sam? What do you want?"

*I've been asking myself that for years.*

"A piece of pecan pie would be nice." He grinned.

She considered him with a steady gaze. "So you do have a secret," she mused. "I can live with that for now." She glanced at her watch. "Oh. I got that thing."

He had nothing to do but return to the single-wide trailer and count the stars. "Book deliveries?"

She rose. "Martha has a hang-up about everyone knowing. I shouldn't have told you." Skylar hiked her purse on her shoulder.

"Martha doesn't have to know."

Skylar fussed with a hoop earring.

"Where are these so-called books anyway?" He logged in every delivery. He couldn't imagine where they were stashed at the bookstore.

"In the nook under the stairs. Behind all the pillows, there's a hidden door. Unless you know it's there, it blends in with the wainscoting."

The nook.

*Where troubles melt away between the pages.*

# SIX

North of Broadmoor, at Butte Junction, Sam traveled off the paved road onto gravel. "You sure this is the right way?"

Skylar motioned ahead. "Not too much farther."

Sam brushed the mess of hair hanging in his eyes and tightened his grip on the steering wheel. The bristlecone pines masked what little light remained along the snaking road. After several hairpin turns, a house appeared. Sam slowed and pulled up behind a Range Rover. Through the dusty windshield, he eyed the estate posing as a cabin hidden in a canopy of pines. Sam couldn't help smiling. Hiding wealth vastly differed from Edward's viewpoint. "We showcase our money, son," his father would say. "Others want what we have, and we have a duty to remind them of what they don't have." *Ridiculous.*

Skylar gathered a manila-wrapped book from the back seat.

"Discreet." Sam raised an eyebrow.

A thread of irritation flashed across her face as she exited the car. She walked to the door. A quick exchange was followed by a handshake.

"Easy peasy," she said once back inside the Buick.

Sam started the engine. "Are we done?" Eyeing the rearview mirror, he backed out and swung the car down the mountain.

"Two more."

On the outskirts of town, she directed him to an Italian restaurant. Cassini's. The parking lot, littered with beer bottles and cigarette butts, led to a darkened entrance. Sam parked, glanced around. It wasn't the safest area.

"Be back in a jiff." Skylar exited the car.

With a hand on the door handle, Sam considered following her inside. *They're books*, he reminded himself. *Just books*. He fidgeted with the side mirror, spotting a tent pitched along the back alley. *What's she up to?*

Sam was thumping the steering wheel when she finally returned. She had a gleam in her eyes and couldn't sit still as if she'd downed a double espresso.

"You really like this delivery business, don't you?"

She adjusted the seat belt strap. "Broadmoor's just a blip on the map. There's a world out there." Her eyes brightened. A fleck of gold he hadn't noticed before flickered in her eyes.

"My travel fix comes Sunday nights. *Mutual of Omaha's Wild Kingdom*," he joked, but she didn't find him funny and grew silent. He cleared his throat and backtracked. "Sounds like you're searching for something you can't find here. Foreign travel?"

She shrugged. "Paris, maybe."

"Wow." His attempt to rally excitement sounded strangled, even to his own ears. Memories of his parents dragging a five-year-old through endless art museums. Gothic beasts winking at him, so it seemed, on canvases twice his size.

"All dreams, of course." Her voice had fallen flat. She settled deeper in the seat, rested her head back, and glanced out the window at the night sky thick with stars.

He had burst her bubble. He sat with that thought for a moment before firing up the car. The warble of worn tires filled the dead air. As they crossed over the Taylor River Bridge, he thought about his place not far upstream. He couldn't imagine showing her his stripped trailer. The life he chose to live was contrary to everything she wanted. Times like these poked doubts in his firm resolve to swear off money. People talked about having a fire in their belly for a certain career or extravagant wants and all that crap. The closest Sam came to that deep-gut feeling involved punishing his father. And that was enough.

"Where now?" He tried to sound upbeat, but honestly, he'd seen enough. He'd fleshed out the real Skylar. No longer the simple, freckled girl in faded jeans, he'd seen her eyes dance and her voice swell with wanting.

Solemnly, she offered directions. Maybe she too had pegged him and wanted the night to end.

Soon they were parked in front of a modest, two-story home. A streetlight flooded the dull-yellow siding and rickety front porch.

Skylar unfolded from the car. Before she could fetch books from the back seat, the screen door squeaked open, and a willowy figure appeared, shadowed beneath the pitch of the porch.

"Is that you, Skylar?"

Skylar straightened and poked her head above the car. "I changed my route tonight!" she yelled. "Sorry to leave you last." She collected two books from the back seat.

Sam eyed Skylar in the rearview mirror. "Who is this guy?"

"I think his name is Cyrus," she whispered. "He's . . . different." She shrugged. "But I like him."

Sam wanted to ask what she meant by "different," but the man had stepped off the porch and was heading toward them. When he stood beside the Buick, his eyes dipped to Sam inside the car before meeting Skylar's eyes. "I have something quite exciting to show you." He stroked his trimmed goatee and glanced at Sam. "You're welcome to join us."

# SEVEN

"Tisha, you don't have to go."

Curbside at her mother's weathered bungalow, Nina plugged the Wilshire Baptist Church address into the GPS. She waited for Tisha to buckle up before signaling and pulling out into traffic.

"Of course I don't have to. I want to."

*To support you.* Why couldn't she have said that?

"Did you know the man?" Tisha asked.

A flicker of sunlight caught the rearview mirror. Nina adjusted it and sucked in a long breath. Going alone to the funeral had seemed daunting. Tisha had won out in Nina's narrow pool of support candidates. And now she regretted it.

"Well?" Tisha waited.

"Not really," Nina admitted. "I heard he had a wife and kids." Why had she divulged that? Maybe it weighed on her, knowing the children had lost their father like she had. The circumstances were different, of course.

"Still has a family," Tisha corrected.

"How can you be so . . ." Nina searched for the kindest word. ". . . flippant, Mother? Someone died." Calling Tisha "Mother" bordered on treason. Something to do with labeling or new birth. Nina rolled her eyes.

"Death happens, Nina." Tisha pulled out a nail file and began working it in short strokes across her pale tips.

"I was there," Nina admitted. "In his room." She bit her lip, wishing she could rewind that day, ignore the incessant ringing, and walk by without a second thought.

"So you finally dumped Bobby." Tisha held up a hand. "Hallelujah. The man exudes negative energy. Never understood what you saw in him."

*Stability, independence, and something else I can't think of right now.* "Bobby was like the others, Mother. Just a distraction. I haven't seen him in six months." She turned to Tisha, near exasperation. Nina wanted to remind her *she had left Dad*. But what good would that do? Tisha's explanations always looped back to a spiritual awakening or something equally asinine.

"What were you doing in the man's room?"

Nina considered turning the car around at the next exit. "It's complicated. Leave it at that."

Soon the GPS announced their arrival. Nina swung into the parking lot and chose a vacant spot a good distance from the stone building perched on a hill. A graveyard flanked the church. *How convenient.*

Tisha tucked the nail file inside her bag. "I wonder if I'll see spirits around the casket." She turned to Nina, fascination lighting her hazel-blue eyes. The same color eyes as Nina, yet Tisha's always held mischief.

Nina felt for pockets to stow her keys and realized she'd worn the black suit jacket without any. "People cremate nowadays," she said offhandedly and reached behind the seat for her purse.

"How do you know?"

*Because on a rainy day last April, I perched on the edge of a stiff chair beside Dad in the ICU listening to the constant beeping sound signaling life. When the blip became solid, a flood of nurses mobilized around him. I witnessed death, Mother. Then life.*

She remembered it all. The moment the intermittent beep returned, like musical notes to her ears. The nurse with kind eyes and a loose ponytail adjusted the drip oozing life back into his body, a mere dimple beneath the white sheet. She handed Nina a drift of papers. "No hurry," she said and turned to leave.

Nina glanced down at the scribble of words.

*Durable Do-Not-Resuscitate Order.*

"Wait," Nina pleaded.

The nurse turned, smiled tightly. She glanced out the door, reminding Nina she had others to attend to. Nina placed her open palm on the top paper, covering the ugly words. "What would you do?" Confusion, lack of sleep, whatever you called it, had muddled her mind.

The nurse hesitated. "I'd sign the DNR." She glanced at the frail man in the bed. "If it's his time, let him go." She tucked the stethoscope she held inside her pocket. "But I think he's a fighter."

Just words, of course, but they filled Nina with hope. She stood, brushed his collarbone peeking out above the blue smock. A weak wash of color had returned to his hollowed cheeks, or maybe she imagined it.

The nurse had closed the door, leaving Nina alone in the cool, sterile room. She glanced over at the papers. He would want her to be prepared. But she couldn't sign them. Not yet.

She rifled through magazines on the shelf affixed to the wall and grabbed one. She dragged a chair closer to the bed. Before opening the magazine, she waited for the thin sheet covering his chest to rise and fall. Satisfied, she flipped through the pages. Not reading. Not really. More something to do.

On the last page, a serene sunset caught her eye. A wash of vibrant yellows and oranges. In the forefront, resting in the sand, sat a pebbled box with a caption below: *Prepare for your loved one. Cremation keeps them close by.*

---

". . . let us go forth in the certain hope of being reunited with Sam Wood at the end of time. Go in God's peace, and may the Almighty bless you now and forevermore."

Nina waited until others stood before using Tisha's arm as a tether and stepping out of the pew in time with the melancholy hymn droning from the organ. The service had drained her. She needed fresh air, a paintbrush, and a drink. She felt no obligation to view the family photos and strayed from the gathering line. In the throng, Tisha managed to slip away and beelined for the guest book.

"You can't sign that," Nina scolded once she caught up to her.

"We've driven all this way." Tisha lifted the readers hung from a beaded chain and affixed them low on her nose. She ran fingertips over the signatures in the guest book.

"What are you doing?" Nina whispered. She glanced around, hoping no one was watching.

"Seeing if I can pick up anything."

Nina gently grasped Tisha's shoulder and backed her away from the Ouija Board.

"Do you feel better now?" Tisha jerked at Nina's grip. "I just wanted to—"

"Head down, Mother," Nina ordered. "Let's get out of here." And that was the plan until Nina dropped the program and it landed beside a polished, low-heeled pump.

Nina bent and quickly confiscated the trifold. When she stood, she was looking into the face of Sam Wood's wife, Odilia.

Nina's breath caught in her throat. For what seemed like minutes, neither of them broke eye contact.

Nina recognized her from the photos on the screen during the slide-show. Much older now than in the photos, her chestnut curls no longer bounced. Extra pounds had stolen her waistline, leaving her chunky where the pictures had showed a firm body. Recent tears had left her pale and puffy. The woman shepherded a boy and a girl, both in those awkward preteen years where their faces hadn't caught up with their bodies.

Nina stood rigid, stone-faced, an attempt to mask any hint of who she was or her connection to Odilia's husband. Yet she wanted to show concern. Something she often failed at. "Sorry for your loss."

Odilia's eyes scanned Nina from head to toe. Her lips held in a thin but smudged penciled line, an awful shade of coral that made her look sickly. "He said you were quite good." She grasped the shawl knotted at her chest with an iridescent opal, stunning and bright against the forlorn, black dress. "There's others here, you know." A slight upward tilt of her chin, she glanced around. "The art community can be generous when you're the wife of someone on the selection committee. Everyone becomes your friend." She offered a tight, awkward smile. "Except you."

Nina tried not to frown. Odilia was clearly angry yet hid it behind a tight smile. Odilia knew. She didn't have to say it. Not here in the church. Yet she did.

"Do you make a habit of drinking with committee members, or do you drink with anyone that comes along?"

Nina was making a fist, trying to slough off her desire to defend herself. It didn't seem right to respond. Not here in a church, regardless of how no response might be perceived.

"Mom, I'm thirsty." The boy, the younger of the two, tugged on his mother's shawl.

Nina glanced at both children. The girl in an ironed A-line and tight curls. The boy's hair wouldn't stay slicked back and fell heavily across his forehead. Both had puffy, downcast eyes. Nina needed them to look up, to see the hurt in their eyes. A punishment perhaps. She felt Odilia's glare and tore away from the children and got the hell out of there.

Outside, a sprinkling of guests had gathered underneath a pergola. Nina sucked in a breath and searched for Tisha. Her mother was a vortex of high energy. Anyone willing to listen received the assurance of life beyond this world. Nina doubted they understood Tisha meant an afterlife where their loved ones were ghosts.

A microphone appeared out of nowhere and was thrust abruptly in her face.

"Martin Shupin, KRDO Channel 13 news."

Nina blinked, held up a hand. She stepped backward.

"I understand you were in the room when Sam Wood died." The stiff-haired reporter touched his ear as if he was being fed information. "Can you tell us about your relationship with Mr. Wood, and are you aware that an autopsy is pending?"

Nina's mouth hung open, vacant of words. In the distance, hitched beside the pergola post, she spotted a cameraman among the knotty vines.

A meaty hand engulfed hers. "We're done here," a baritone voice announced. The hand jerked her sideways.

Almost losing a shoe, she hurried in tow, clapping along the courtyard pavers to a side entrance leading back into the church. The stranger quickly keyed the lock. Nina snuck a nervous glance over her shoulder before being dragged inside what looked like a storage room.

"My mother?" she asked, biting her lip.

"The office will find her." He dug out a phone from his baggy shorts and began texting.

Nina tried to shake off the tension in her shoulders. *Who is this guy?* She didn't feel threatened. Still. "You came along at the right time." She fiddled with the purse strap biting into her shoulder.

The man pocketed the phone. Hands on hips, he faced the wall of shelves. "Baptism's tonight at Teen Club." He hauled a box off the bottom shelf, seemingly uninterested in what had just happened.

Being hijacked, even if for a good cause, left her unsettled. She placed a hand across her churning belly. "I'm Nina," she offered. "I guess I should thank you." She couldn't help spying the door, expecting a reporter. *Autopsy.* The word rattled inside her mouth with nowhere to go.

"Should I go find my mother?" She was frazzled. What if the reporter had wrangled Tisha? Who knew what she would tell him. Her playful gene often devolved into blatant jabber. Nina cringed. *Mother, where are you?*

"Let's give it a few minutes." He had a calm voice or maybe he didn't care. She couldn't tell which. He lumbered over to a sink, hose in tow. After fastening the nozzle, he dragged the hose across the room.

"So, this is what you do for a living?" She always thought in those terms. What you did was singed into your being, an identity for life.

Like her painting. Her path didn't deviate. She was and would always be a painter, like her father.

"Nope. Just a servant of God."

*Wait till Tisha gets wind of this,* she thought as he hefted the lid off a sea-blue crate and dipped the hose inside a hot tub on wheels. He turned on the water and leaned against the tub. For the first time, he looked at her. "This is something I do to pass time." He shrugged. "When I have patients, I check their eyes. You know, 'Which is better, one or two?'"

"An optometrist?"

He nodded and swished a hand under the steady stream flowing into the tub. "I sat fairly close to you inside." He lifted his chin toward the sanctuary. "You were rubbing your eyes quite a bit. Are they bothering you?" He wiped a wet hand against his worn cargo shorts.

"My eyes?" She blinked, thinking this must be optometrist small talk. "They're sensitive to light. That's all."

"Any dryness, blurred vision?"

She bristled. "Maybe something got in my eye." She turned toward the door, then back to the man.

He strolled over, handed her a card. "If you ever want your eyes checked out, I'd be happy to take a peek."

Nina looked into his eyes: summer blue, slightly squinted, vacant of something she couldn't put her finger on. She glanced down at the card. "Dr. Frank."

"Jack Frank." He chuckled. "I know. Two first names." He had a craggy smile, a sun-scorched complexion, lined and plain tired.

"Parents can be cruel," she mused.

The door from the sanctuary opened, a blaze of light backlighting Tisha. "Speaking of cruel parents," Nina mumbled.

"I thought they'd carted you off to the poky, handcuffs and all." A fierce fire shimmered in Tisha's eyes and something else. A glimmer of worry.

Confused, Jack looked at Nina. "Jail?"

"Word is she killed Sam Wood in his hotel room." Tisha scooted past Jack as if she owned the place.

# EIGHT

héret's whimsical theater prints needed a new home. Working part time at The Art Loft kept Nina busy. Lately, she'd tackled every half-baked idea Stacey, the owner, had suggested. Two weeks had passed since Sam Wood's demise. Joan, or whomever the collective "we" was that she had mentioned, had not called. Nina couldn't take the suspense much longer.

Nina unhooked the prints and hefted the sturdy frames to another vignette. After hanging them, she returned the hammer and assortment of nails to the closet. She glanced around, let out a breath. Now what? Honestly, she was beat.

So far, she'd managed to drown out the possibility of bad news. Would Joan and the committee strip her of Best of Show? Would they ban her from participating in future events or blackball her altogether? Crap. She'd failed at the whole distraction thing. And still, she was looking over her shoulder for Kanoy. She thought she had seen him when she had popped into Pie-pie for a bite before work. Most of The Galleries shop staff frequented the restaurant. Apparently, cops too. But this one, holed up in a booth and hunched over one of Piper's delicious potpies, had a goatee and a pleasant smile.

Nina walked the gallery in search of another project, thinking about how she loved her job. Discussing art with clients coughing up big bucks was surreal at times. The experience stimulated something cerebral, visceral. Highbrow conversations about the artists' intent or their color choices kept her focused on her own goals. She was proud of her paintings. If their beauty didn't catch someone's eyes, she hoped her perseverance would shine through in her technique. Neither were enough, though. She wanted awards. She wanted her paintings in galleries and hanging in someone's living room.

Stacey had posted a sign in the window: *Resident artist Nina Shubert showing here soon.* If a customer wavered on a sale, Nina would point out the sign. A last-ditch offer to reel them back in or at the least pin them inside the gallery long enough to listen to her spiel.

*My technique is wet-on-wet watercolor. I paint quirky subjects, things you'd see at home like an unkempt bed of wrinkled sheets or a spent tube of toothpaste resting on the sink.*

Interesting, right?

The doorbell chimed. As Nina breezed past the front windows, she caught a glimpse of the sign. Her gut ached. Three years, and Stacey had never asked Nina to show her work.

The glass door swung open. Nina rallied a smile as two curly-haired girls wearing yellow slickers bounded through the door and stomped their galoshes, making a whacking sound on the painted cement.

"Morgan, Mallory, umbrellas down. Inside rules, remember." Stacey, wearing yoga pants and a zippered jacket, ushered her girls over to a bench seat. "I can handle snow," she said to Nina. "But rain drives me batty." She plucked several books and two ratty-haired

Barbies from a backpack. "Off to the lounge," she ordered and tapped the girls' damp shoulders, prodding them along.

Seeing Stacey weighed down with backpacks, a tote, and umbrellas, Nina offered a hand. "Got it." Stacey trekked to a desk neatly tucked at the back of the gallery. Nina followed. "More projects?" God, she hoped so.

"I can't have them coming around." Stacey pinned Nina with a solemn face. "It's not good for business."

"What are you talking about?"

"Reporters." Stacey frowned. "Sarah had two skulking at the door when she opened this morning. And . . ." She paused. "One called me at home." She settled in the chair and waved the cordless mouse.

Nina was digesting what she'd heard as the laptop sprang to life. A few clicks, and the work shift spreadsheet appeared. Stacey began deleting Nina's name from the schedule. No edge of concern, no questions on why reporters were there. Nothing. Stacey had only one mode: business. Nina thought of how she had treated Fanny. No encouraging words. No kind smile. Maybe she was that way too. It served a purpose, of course. Until it didn't.

Stacey swiveled in the chair. "Two weeks." She looked expectant. It didn't sound like a question. "You'll let me know?"

*What? Whether I killed the man?* Nina solemnly nodded. She retrieved her purse from the bottom desk drawer. How could this be happening? She looked at Stacey, unamused by her punishing action. A dose of scorn followed, but she hid that behind a brief smile.

Outside, she stormed to the car. A parking ticket was tucked underneath the windshield wiper. *Great.* Nina ripped it off, glanced at the violation. Street-sweeping day. She grunted. With a tug, she opened the car door and flung the ticket inside. She wanted to go home, drink straight from the bottle, and paint herself into oblivion.

—————

Cabernet sloshed in a tumbler. At least she'd used a glass. For that reason, she toasted herself and enjoyed a generous sip. Turning to the palette, she mopped up violet and dragged a paintbrush across the wet paper already fused with yellows and oranges. A sunset. Not her usual medley of cream colors. Alcohol, she'd learned, championed courage.

The phone rang.

"Am I calling too late?" Joan's sickeningly sweet voice.

Nina dropped the brush in water. "No, of course not." Opening her eyes wide, she fought to speak reasonably through the cabernet fog. "I was painting." Pleased with that fact, she left her cozy art closet and traversed the snug living room to the kitchen. She went to cork the bottle and missed the bottle altogether.

"We received a blurb about the incident."

*That's what they're calling it?*

"Incident," Nina repeated, hoping she didn't slur the word.

"Yes. With Sam Wood."

Hearing his name, Nina immediately sobered up. "Am I in trouble?" She grasped the quartz counter. She wanted the bottom line. She'd waited long enough—her whole life, in fact—to get a Best of Show. And it had been a long haul of hundreds of planned steps: classes, practice, lectures, diving into the art community, and pretending to like everyone and everything.

"Nothing's definitive," Joan said.

It should have been a relief. Instead, Nina's stomach soured.

"We'll revisit the incident in a few months. By then . . ." Joan's voice faded.

*By then what?* She'd be in prison. Was that what the committee thought? That she had killed him?

"I didn't harm Mr. Wood, if that's what you're thinking." There, she'd said it. And it wasn't the alcohol talking.

"It's late." Joan's voice had tightened. "An official letter will be sent soon. Take care."

Nina ended the call, slid the phone across the countertop, and collared the wine bottle.

For three days, she marinated in her apartment. Turned out Thai, chicken wings, and sweet pickles from the fridge paired nicely with whiskey. Tonight, though, she wasn't particularly hungry. After flipping through TV channels, she highjacked the bottle and settled into her art space: a desk built into the linen closet off the hallway. To combat the cramped, dark space, she'd paid a bundle for full-spectrum lighting. She still didn't understand the technology, but it worked.

She clicked on the light and blinked a few times. A weathered can of brushes and creased and contorted paint tubes crowded one side of the desk. Fingertips grazed the sharpened pencils, the bottles of ink on the other side. Assorted sponges, discolored and tough, held faded colors like memories of past paintings. Of course, she kept all those canvases stacked on shelves, hidden in drawers.

Centered on the desk sat the half-finished sunset over *Garden of the Gods*. She'd started the painting three drunks ago. Slipping into the chair, she settled into the sweet spot: enough elbow room, but not too close to the table. There.

She dipped a thick brush into the speckled water cup, swirled. A heaviness pressed down on her. The brush felt awkward in her hand, her grip all wrong. Imaginary or not, she struggled to lift the brush and felt betrayed by her own mind. She reached for a different brush, a mop brush. Dunking it hastily in the water, she dipped it in cerulean blue. The color appeared too weak or too strong. Too something.

It was as if she had never painted before or she was painting with her left hand. Many times, she'd lost motivation, strayed from her regimen. She always rebounded, often fiercer than before. Never *this*. She slumped back in the chair.

The phone beeped. A text from Bobby. He wanted to reconnect. Ugh. Working quick fingers, she claimed she had a cold. He wouldn't want to listen to her problems. Lines had been drawn long ago. Convenience triumphed over commitment.

The phone beeped again. Tisha. *Downstairs. Popping in for a visit.* Not a common occurrence. Ugh.

Shrugging into a robe, Nina scoured the condo for evidence. After ditching two empty wine bottles, she spied the whiskey decanter. Snagging the fancy bottle, she returned it to the bar cart. In the bathroom. she ran a dry toothbrush across her teeth. Good enough.

Nina opened the door a smidgen. "Hello, Tisha." She hadn't decided if she was going to let her in.

"Don't you look cozy." Tisha pushed past Nina, drifted into the kitchen, and upended the contents of a bag onto the counter. "Saint John's Wort." She rattled the bottle, the noise bringing an instant ache to Nina's temple. From her coat pocket, Tisha produced red, polished stones and held them in her open palm. "Jasper. They're action stones." She reached out, expecting Nina to take them.

Short of rolling her eyes, Nina begrudgingly picked up the stones.

"They help with ambition." Tisha punched the empty bag into her hippie purse. "That's the problem, right?"

Not even close. Nina held the stones like dice. Was it that obvious that something was off? She shot a look at her mother. *How did she know I couldn't paint?* Nina tossed the stones on the counter and picked up the bottle of Saint John's Wort. She squinted at the label.

"I'll try these." She figured she owed Tisha a twinge of interest in her potions. She had, after all, come over. That was something.

"Perfect." Tisha embraced her daughter, a rare display of affection. She stepped back, looked at Nina critically. "Do something with that hair. And your breath." She started toward the door. "You know there're natural remedies for halitosis."

"Goodbye, Mother."

When the door closed, Nina dumped the bottle and the stones in the trash. The doorbell chimed again.

"Mother," she groused. Tightening the floppy belt on her robe, she stomped to the door.

Flash. Flash.

Nina raised a hand, sheltered her eyes from the bright light.

"Becca Barker, KKTV Channel 11." The petite blonde huddled beside a man hoisting a camera. "Ms. Shubert." Polished lips held a weak smile. "We've just heard that the autopsy results for Sam Wood should be available next week."

Nina's face dropped. There was that word again. *Autopsy*. It wasn't a tongue twister unless you said it several times. With a firm shove, Nina closed the door. The thud echoed, worsening her headache. Her connection to Sam Wood's death was officially out of control. Her gut revolted. Nausea came in waves. She hurried to the bathroom. For the first time in forever, she couldn't ask her father what to do.

# 1985

# NINE

If Sam didn't see another book for the rest of his life, he would be fine with that. Martha decided to switch the folk and fairy-tale sections with picture books. Sam lugged books back and forth the entire shift.

When Martha left, claiming a headache, Sam seized the opportunity. Cradling a healthy slice of her pastry du jour—carrot cake—on a napkin, he moseyed over to the nook and camped against the pillows, hoping no one would find him. Two bites in, he pulled away from the wall. Something was poking his ribs. A Hot Wheels-size car nestled between the pillows. When Sam reached for the car, the wall moved. A faint click sounded, and a door quivered open. Skylar had said it was near invisible, blending into the wainscoting on the walls.

"Huh." Sam tossed the pillows aside and peered inside. He smiled. He loved this kind of thing. After a quick glance back toward the hallway and seeing no one, Sam inched his way inside the room until he could stand.

Sealed boxes cluttered the unfinished floor. And a table, chair, and lamp. Only bare studs defined the dimly lit room. Sam recognized today's shipment perched closest to the door. He didn't want to mess with that one. Too obvious if the box was opened and books were missing. He crouched beside an older box behind the table. Using a car key, he slit through the tape.

Voices drifted in. He froze.

Creeping toward the door, wincing every time his knees met the floorboards, Sam quietly pulled the door closed. He waited, listened, his chest thumping in a good way, pure exhilaration.

Finally, the voices passed. Making his way back to the box, Sam hefted two—no, three—books from it. He didn't bother to read the titles. It didn't matter. He knew they were rare and would fetch a few bucks.

———————

By the end of the day, Sam was starved. And probably smelly. He ached for a shower. His stomach, however, nixed the idea.

Before dropping off book orders with Skylar, Sam had never noticed Cassini's, the Italian restaurant. Now every time he passed the garish sign with a brazen bombshell holding clumps of grapes, his curiosity spiked. Between that and his hunger, Sam swerved into the parking lot. As soon as he stepped out of the car, the waft of tomato sauce teased his taste buds. A bite of brisk air followed him down the slope to the entrance. He should have worn a jacket.

Inside, a sprinkling of tables held diners. Families, mostly. A catchy Italian song whispered beneath the low lights. Sam considered leaving. Not his vibe.

A waiter paraded by carrying a plate of cheesy who knows what. Sam's belly nudged him forward, and he followed the guy. Before the waiter slipped out the back entrance, Sam folded into a booth with a window looking out onto the patio. No patrons had chosen the patio despite the cozy firepit.

That waiter, however, came into view and plopped onto a patio chair. Looking far more spent than Sam, which was saying something, the fellow slid low, tugged the bill of his cap covering his eyes, and rested against the chair back, ignoring altogether the steaming dinner he'd carried out there.

Sam, near salivating, ordered the same meal when a waitress swooped in. "I'll have what he's having." Sam tipped his head toward the window.

Waiting to eat alone proved unbearable. He didn't want people staring at him. He kept glancing out the window. A game of sorts ensued. Would the guy dive into the parm, no doubt shortly becoming a frozen dinner?

Sam's meal arrived. He'd had chicken parmesan before. This, though, rocked his world. Ignoring the pangs in his gut and his primal desire to wolf it down, Sam ate politely. Savoring the last bite, he swiped the cloth napkin across his lips. Meeting the waitress's eyes, he signaled for the bill. While digging for his wallet, Sam finally caught the guy outside eating. A fork in one hand and a book in the other, he shoveled it in. All the while, his gaze remained glued to the open book on the table.

Sam left cash and moseyed out to the patio. Why he had the need to spark a conversation, he wasn't sure. He spoke to kids all day. Well, not really. He would drift into the kitchen to avoid them. Skylar and the other girls interested him. Even that, though, had its limitations. So why was he going outside? It was damned cold.

The blaze from the firepit warmed his cheeks. He stood close, lapping up the warmth. "The food's good here." Sam rallied a smile, rubbed his hands together over the flames. "Great, actually."

The guy tore away from the book, glanced up at Sam. He looked perturbed or at least confused.

Sam felt a need to fill up the awkwardness. "Yeah, I saw you walk by with that." He pointed at the guy's near-empty plate.

"Chicken parmesan," he deadpanned, scooped a generous bite onto his fork and returned to the book.

Sam nodded, feeling stupid now for bothering him. It was obvious he didn't want company. Yet Sam stepped closer. He was cold, the fire inviting. The propane feeding the fire whirred, making a conversation of its own.

A burst of flame illuminated the book cover. "What are you reading?" Sam asked. It dawned on him then, as if the arc of light dancing onto the book was telling him something. Could the book be from Skylar's deliveries?

"A girl book." He flipped the book over as if he'd forgotten the title. He read it slowly. "*The Edible Woman*." He smiled. "First edition."

It did look girly. Pink cover with a cartoonish picture of a woman. "First edition?" Sam brightened. It had to be one of Skylar's. Feeling emboldened, he sat down across from him. "I work with Skylar." Sam's eyes dropped to the book. "What's the allure of this one?"

The man straightened in the chair. Dimples the size of quarters framed his grin. He rattled off what he had learned about collecting rare books and selling them. Fascination awakened his rather dull, wide-set eyes.

"This," he held up the pink cover, "is going to get me out of this job." On face value, a guy with oodles of inky-black hair and an athletic build holding up a cartoonlike pink book appeared comical.

Sam wasn't laughing.

Another scrape across the plate, mopping up the last puddle of sauce. "Later, I get to clean this plate." He was shaking his head. He dropped the fork on the plate. An obvious exclamation point to his disdain.

Sam could relate. "I shuffled books around the store today. Like it mattered where the fairy-tale books were."

"Same circus, you and me."

Sam had never considered Martha's special book orders anything more than fancy books people placed in cabinets and pulled out once a year to admire. "What do you think you can get for it, say a year from now?" Sam, tapping a finger on the table, imagined him calculating numbers in his head as his eyes darted side to side.

"At least a thousand. Paid two bills."

Even his dad would think this book business was brilliant. And Cyrus. Telling Cyrus held more appeal. He would applaud Sam, ask questions like he really wanted to know what Sam was interested in.

Sam smiled. "That much, huh? I'm Sam."

"Luca."

They both nodded. A spark from the fire illuminated Luca's features, making him appear like a doe in the headlights. Low-hanging fruit.

Sam snapped his eyes off the book and tucked his hands in his pockets. "Any desserts worth trying?"

It was easy really. Luca hustled off to the kitchen to bring his new buddy a cannoli. Chef's special, he claimed. What was special was that Luca had left the book on the table.

Sam snapped it up, untucked his shirt, and stuck the book inside his waistband.

# TEN

O nce the reporter had left last night around 10:00 p.m., Nina had slumped on the sofa and intended to only close her eyes. Around 4:00 a.m., she awoke, startled. Brushing sleep from her eyes, she peered through the peephole. No distorted figures lurked outside. After hustling into clothes, she slipped out of the apartment.

Nina parked in a strip mall. Gray clouds filled the sky, a backdrop to the bleak L-shaped building asleep with the rest of the town. She cranked the key again and ran the heater, wiggling her toes. Warm clothes—clothes that matched, even—hadn't crossed her mind.

She'd been parked for thirty minutes. With the heater on, her toes inside the spongy slippers finally had warmed. She turned off the car and flipped over the business card on her lap. Three doors down from the Foodmart, she spotted Monument Optical. The *O* was missing or faded. She couldn't tell which.

Cold seeped into her bones. Or was it desperation? She wanted her life back. Not even a week had passed since Joan had suspended her designation, and yet the loss sat heavy in Nina's chest. She missed the quirky vibe of the gallery, sharing her art chops with the lookie-loos. Mostly, she missed painting. Still, she struggled. Finally, she had cleared off the desk so she wouldn't haven't to be reminded of her failure.

Earlier, after leaving her apartment, she had slowed past Tisha's house and considered seeking refuge there. The car had pushed on like it had a mind of its own. After driving through a twenty-four-hour joint for tea, she had pulled out Jack's business card. Maybe that had been her intention all along.

Around 7:00 a.m., a dribble of vehicles began to arrive in the strip mall. Tired workers unfolded from cars, some lighting up for a quick fix, others pinning name tags on prim aprons before dragging into the grocery store. When a faded-blue truck sputtered into the lot and parked in front of Monument Optical, she straightened, zipped her sweatshirt, and pocketed the car keys.

Jack exited the rust bucket and stooped to tie his sneakers. Nina sucked in a nervous breath and opened the car door. He stood with his back to her, patting his pockets as if checking for a wallet.

"Jack!" she called out.

He turned, and his eyebrows knit together. A glint of sun had broken through the clouds, lighting his wet hair. As she drew closer, wrinkles danced across his forehead. And a scar she hadn't noticed in the church snaked through one eyebrow.

A moment passed before dawning tugged at his lips. "Church lady?"

"Yes." She played with the zipper at her neck. "You said to stop by, get my eyes checked." A nervous chuckle escaped.

Jack scratched the stubble mapping his cheek and glanced over at the office. "I have patients at eight." He winced. "I've got maybe ten minutes."

Inside the exam room painted a robin's egg blue, she perched on the cushy seat armed with the unwieldy apparatus used to test eyesight. A warped Formica countertop flanked one wall. A mish-mash of contact lens boxes were stacked on the counter, waiting for someone to organize the lot. The room appeared uncared for, including the discolored eye chart at the far side of the room. Covering one eye, she was trying to read the letters when Jack strolled in carrying two Styrofoam cups. "Coffee?"

She took the cup.

"So." He blew on the steaming coffee and sat on the low swivel chair in front of her. "I'm thinking this visit has nothing to do with your eyes."

She breathed in mocha, wishing she liked coffee. "Do you remember what my mother said at the church?" When he looked confused, Nina immediately felt embarrassed. She didn't want to repeat Tisha's comment. "It's ridiculous how rumors start. And this one . . ." She swallowed a sip and made a face as the pungent liquid trickled down her throat. "People think I murdered a man."

Her words hung in the air. Jack shuffled his feet, walking the chair to the counter. He set the cup down before looking at her. Maybe he wanted to say something, but his lips didn't move.

"I didn't do anything," she blurted. "I'm afraid the—"

"Police?" he tossed out like he was answering a question.

"Yes," she nodded. "I mean no." She closed her eyes. "The police interrogated me in the hotel. There was nothing to tell them, really." Thinking about it now, she could only recall snippets of the time in Sam Wood's room. Could she have missed something?

"I, ah, don't know much about the law." Jack shrugged.

She sat waiting for more. Nothing came. "I shouldn't have come." That much was obvious. Unloading on him seemed like a horrible idea.

He swiped a slow hand across his chin. "You seem like a nice woman, and I can see you're upset. Understandably so." He reached for his coffee. "Listen, anyone who would wait in the butt cold near dawn to talk to me deserves more than ten minutes."

She fought to hide her relief, yet she wondered what exactly she expected from him. He couldn't make the accusation disappear, bring Sam Wood back to life, or dismiss the nagging feeling there was something else. Something right before her eyes. Something she might have done. But what? That thought lingered like a bad taste in her mouth.

# ELEVEN

A fish tank anchored the far wall in Jack's otherwise drab back office. Nina, fascinated by a fish hovering near the bottom, watched the stream of bubbles floating to the surface. After that ran its course, she sank into one of the chairs and checked her phone for messages. Nothing.

Twenty minutes later, Jack bounded into the room. "Still here. Great." He dragged a chair beside hers and pulled two granola bars from his shirt pocket.

She shook her head. She couldn't eat. He unwrapped a bar, inhaled a bite, and looked at her expectantly as if to say, "Go."

And like a dam breaking, she spilled every detail she could remember of that afternoon in the hotel. Even a few more details. Maybe that was what she had needed. A stranger to sift through fresh facts. Someone without preconceived ideas about her occasional drinking. Or someone who wouldn't question why she didn't do more to help the poor guy in the chair.

When she finished, Jack settled back in the chair and laced his hands together. "Well, did you do it?"

She shot him the same look she wielded at her mother whenever she brought up one of her cockamamie cures. "Of course not." Nina looked away. She couldn't believe he'd asked that.

"All I'm saying is things happen in panic situations." He leaned forward. "The mind is tricky. Maybe there's a detail you've forgotten without even knowing it."

"Not possible. I couldn't have forgotten about killing someone." She stood. "Next you're going to tell me to visit a shrink." She hadn't expected the conversation to slide in this direction.

She tossed him an angry glare and padded to the fish tank, again fascinated by the fish. The serpentine scales of the bottom dweller shimmered. A shame really. Nowhere for the fish to go, trapped in the tight space.

"Do I need a lawyer?" She turned to him, held her breath. It seemed unbelievable she had to ask.

"You haven't been charged with anything. Getting a lawyer tells them you have something to hide."

She shook her head. "All because I walked into a room." Like the fish, she felt trapped. Nowhere to go. Barred from the gallery and literally unable to paint. Everything always looped back to painting.

She returned to the seat beside him. "I can't remember a time when I didn't paint." The thought shifted her mind, away from Sam Wood. At least momentarily. "My dad said the first thing I held was a paintbrush."

"I wish I could paint," Jack reflected. He stretched his legs.

"Have you ever tried?" Nina busied her hands in her lap.

"I faintly remember getting one of those paint-by-number sets as a kid." He chuckled. "A horse or something like that."

"For me, it began with a book. My father made me paint every picture in that book. Or at least it seemed that way." She hadn't thought about that book in years. "Started with a picture of a bowl of ice cream."

"Sounds like you spent a lot of time with your dad."

Memories flooded back. Sitting on her knees. Was it at the dinette? She didn't remember. Clumsy hands held a brush and laid timid strokes over the pencil outline her father had sketched.

"Have you told him about what happened?"

"That's not possible." She rose, slung her purse over her shoulder. She hadn't told anybody about what had happened to her father.

"I'm sorry."

"What?" Nina was staring at the fish. "You know your bottom dweller hasn't moved?" She pointed.

Jack walked to the tank and tapped the glass. "Huh? Maybe he's playing dead." He turned to Nina. "Wow." He rubbed his forehead. "That came out wrong."

How could she be mad at him? She barely knew the man, and he had made time for her. Being there was a nice distraction. She shifted to the fish. "Does he have a name?"

"You name fish?" Jack's eyes twinkled. He was joking, of course.

"Pets get names, Jack. I name my paintings."

Jack considered the fish. "You called him 'bottom dweller.' BD." He thought for a moment. "Bob Dylan."

She liked that name. "Bob Dylan it is." She pulled out her keys. It was time to leave. "You've been kind enough to speak with me. I'm not good with people," she admitted. "Thank you."

"People?" He frowned.

"I'm comfortable with a paintbrush in my hand or telling people why they should invest in art." She shrugged.

"Where will you go?" He walked her down the hall to the reception area.

"My mother's." Where else could she go? "I'd like to find that book my dad gave me." After what she'd been through, reliving memories would be a distraction. Maybe even inspire her to paint again. Not the goals she'd been striving for. At this point, she would take anything.

He held open the door. Awkwardly, she slipped past him, feeling his breath feathering her cheek. She began walking to the car.

"You'll come back for an eye exam?" she heard him say. She didn't turn back.

# TWELVE

Nina stood at Tisha's door. "Is the guest room available?" she asked soberly and averted her eyes from Tisha to the mailbox, a zen blue, dotted with stars.

Tisha's mouth opened and then promptly closed. The slightest uptick of an eyebrow followed. "Crystals are strewn across the guest bed. An order arrived yesterday." It wasn't an excuse. More of a warning. Nina despised her mother's interest in spiritual healing. Especially her love of crystals.

Inside Tisha began gathering the pocket-size plastic bags off the bed and moving them to a bamboo credenza below the window. Low and broad, candles adorned the credenza like some sort of altar.

Nina gathered the last few bags and laid them next to the others. She avoided this room where all the hocus-pocus happened. Today, with the sunlight streaming in through the bay window, the room appeared welcoming. She turned to her mother. "The room's perfect."

"Don't mind the . . ." Tisha made circles in the air and pointed at the credenza, "Nothing too alarming, I hope. Unless you light a candle and forget to blow it out."

"No chance of that," Nina assured her and sat on the edge of the bed, testing the firmness with a light bounce.

"The amethyst by the bed will help you sleep."

*Sleep.* "That sounds wonderful." Seeing the glimmer in her mother's eyes, she clarified. "*Sleep* sounds wonderful." She could care less about the gemstone.

"Blankets are in the bottom drawers." Tisha tapped the dresser and padded out of the room.

"Remember that book Dad had?" Nina asked.

Tisha turned, raised an eyebrow. "Dad had many books. Which one?"

"Those boxes I brought over after . . ." Nina looked away, out the window. A bird sat atop a wiry hedge of shrubs outside. Like Tisha, the bird seemed to be waiting for her to say something. The exact something that had happened when Nina had visited her father six months ago. She swallowed. "You know." But Tish didn't. No one knew what Nina did.

"They're exactly where you left them: the mudroom closet. I see them every time I pull out the vacuum." She grimaced. "What joy." Whether or not her intent was to ridicule her father and his books, Nina took it that way. The familiar sentiment proved a constant riff between them. "You're welcome to them. In fact, take them to your place."

"I'm staying away for a bit. Hopefully here. Reporters camped at my door last night."

Tisha's forehead wrinkled. "About you being in Sam Wood's room?"

"Mother," Nina groused.

Sleep didn't come easy. She missed her apartment. Her art. She thought about *The Kiss* by Klimt hanging above her desk. Shimmers of gold. Two heads embracing. Hands entwined. Flowers at their feet. Bobby, the last distraction in her life, had bought the print. At the time, Nina had researched the painting. *The Kiss* involved erotic love, two people merging toward something cosmic. Neither of which she had shared with Bobby. She did love the print, but it reminded her of what was missing in their relationship, in her life. Nina rolled onto her other side. She would take the print down as soon as she returned to her apartment. With that settled, she wrapped the covers over her shoulders and closed her eyes.

Nina awoke to darkness. She reached for the bedside lamp. In the bright light, the quarter-size amethyst seemed to wink at her. She rolled her eyes and padded to the kitchen.

She snuck a few grapes from the fridge and nabbed a handful of crackers before heading to the mudroom. Nina ate the last few Wheat Thins before rolling out the vacuum. There they were. Four stacked boxes. Just as she had left them. A flutter stole her breath. She remembered the day she had emptied her father's bookshelves. A mingle of dust and bourbon had filled her nostrils. Every book had held a piece of him: art, ancient history, botany, and everything in between. She had wanted the books at her place but couldn't bear the daily reminder of what had happened. Of what she had done to her father.

"You'll need these." Tisha stood behind Nina, holding scissors. "You want company?"

Nina briefly smiled and dragged the step stool from the closet. Tisha hunkered on the top rung, her knees jutting out, showing her hippie socks. "What's in that one?" She pointed.

Nina slit the box open. Cocking her head, she read the spines. *"The Masters: Monet, Rembrandt, Renoir."* She slid the box off to the side.

Of course, the book she wanted rested in the final box: *Watercolor Still Life.* She plucked the bright-blue spine with yellow letters and held the weight of it in her lap. Almost giddy, she couldn't wait to thumb through the pages and relive her childhood. When her fingertips traced the yellow letters, they burned. She lifted her hand, confused. The sensation quickly passed, and she wondered if she had imagined it. She glanced at her mother as if she somehow had something to do with it, which, of course, was ridiculous.

"That's the book?" Tisha hadn't noticed the strange occurrence.

A dull tingle still pulsed through Nina's fingers. "Hmm." She held the other hand above the book. Hesitantly, she smoothed her palm across the curvy vase of white trumpet lilies on the cover and braced for another jolt. Nothing. Instead, a memory of her father flooded her thoughts.

*"Why are they droopy, Dad?" Tiny hands fought to hold the book upright.*

*"They've been waiting for you to cheer them up."*

The memory should have brought a smile. Instead, she felt confused by what had happened when she had first touched the book. It must have shown on her face.

Tisha cleared her throat. "Sibby next door ordered smoky quartz. She's a night owl like me. That son-in-law of hers has been asking too many questions about Sibby's finances." She stood. "Smoky quartz should do the trick. Think I'll mosey over."

# THIRTEEN

When Nina heard the front door close, she opened the book. She turned the paint-splattered pages, recalling her father's instruction to a six-year-old who would, frankly, rather have been playing with dolls. Thumbnail sketches he had painted to show her how to paint filled the margins. Awkward strokes, all the colors of the rainbow, marched along the bottom of the pages. Practice, her father had called it. *See if you can mix the exact same color.* With his chair angled toward hers, he squirted colors onto the palette. *Try adding this shade.*

Her love affair with art had begun on these pages.

*See the light edging the cup.*

*She wrestled her father's hand away, dipped his finger in cerulean blue, and pressed his fingertip on the page. She giggled.*

The faint-blue ridges still stained the glossy page. Nina rested her palm over the thumbprint, cementing her touch with his. She could almost feel him next to her. She breathed in mint from the candy he had chewed. And a faint trace of cloves from his cigars.

She continued flipping pages. Smiles came, followed by sadness. That father who had taught her everything about painting no longer existed. Her heart ached. She looked away, wishing she could go back to before the accident. To the inky darkness of that night on the carpet where she had sat stroking his arm. Blame washed over her. For what she had done. No. For what she *hadn't* done.

One fat tear slid down her cheek. She swiped it away. A deep breath followed before she was able to turn the page. Memories awakened and coursed through her. She remembered sitting on her knees, swirling brushes in water, the water making a whirlpool of purple. She saw herself searching out her father's eyes. *Daddy, look at the color I made.* Abruptly, the image vanished.

Now, staring at the last page, the strange burning in her fingertips returned. Slowly at first, like an iron warming up. Nina lifted her hands, examined her fingers, expecting to find an obvious reason for the sensation. A cut, a bite of some sort, redness. Nothing. She rubbed her fingers as if this somehow would alleviate the odd warmth. She wasn't like her mother. She didn't believe in phantom pain. Your inner energy can get out of whack, Tisha would say.

Back to the book. A yellow sticky note rested cockeyed on the page. Nina squinted. Something was written on the back side. A part of her was afraid to touch it. Afraid of the burning. Her hand hovered above the note.

Ridiculous. She rolled her eyes and, with a quick rip, she removed the note like pulling off a Band-Aid.

# FOURTEEN

*he's better than you, Cy. Talent skips a generation. Don't I know.
Focus on her. SW*

Nina frowned. Who the hell was SW? Her father's art
edged on brilliant. Proof hung in his hallway; a piece she'd named
*Paris Bench*. Or had he named it? Either way, it was the spark to
her fascination with painting. Sitting cross-legged in the hall, spine
pressed against the wood paneling, she would stare up at *Paris Bench*
for what seemed like hours. Too young to know why. Only that she
loved the painting her father had made.

She padded to the bedroom, book in hand, hopped on the bed
and opened to the back of the book. To the note.

SW. It dawned on her then.

*Oh my God.*

She leaned in closer. The letters seemed to pulse on the page.

*SW*

*Sam Wood?*

*It's him. Who else could it be? How many people could Dad have
known with those initials?*

The front door squeaked. Nina carefully closed the book and tucked it in her lap. She could feel her heartbeat, steady and strong.

"Enjoying your nostalgia?" Tisha stood in the archway leading into the bedroom, holding Tupperware.

"What did you score?" Nina asked cheerfully, aware of the note as if the book was transparent and she could see through to the last page. Her hands shifted over the book cover.

"Chicken piccata. Enough for two, I'm sure."

"Maybe later." Nina tightened her grip on the spine, sealing the pages for another time. For half a second, she considered showing her mother. But she knew Tisha. A spark of mischief and tomfoolery would ensue if she showed her the note. This wasn't a game. This book represented her memories with her father. And frankly, the note scared her.

Though she had never said it, Nina was certain Tisha resented her relationship with her father. If Nina had adored crystals and all that foolishness, she wondered if things would have been different. A child didn't think like that when they were small. Taking a shine to painting wasn't a parental preference. She hadn't chosen her father over her mother. And she wished Tisha understood that.

"I'm going to the condo in the morning. See if I can sneak inside and pack some clothes." That wasn't the real reason.

"You want company? I could be the lookout." Tisha's eyes lit with mischief.

"I have a few errands too." Nina rested the book beside the bed, considering it for a moment. "I might be gone most of the day." She yawned, crawled up onto the bed. "I'm going back to sleep." Her gaze fell to the Tupperware. "Save me a sliver?"

Knowing she'd disappointed her mother, Nina blew her a kiss. Something she hadn't done since she was a child. More often than not, those playful kisses had been directed at her father. Then again, he was the one who had tucked her in at bedtime.

# FIFTEEN

A drive often cleared Nina's thoughts. Especially when a jumble of problems stalled a painting project.

The notion her father had known Sam Wood implicated her. Or at least implicated her father. Caught in the room with a dead man she didn't know was bad enough. Now there was a viable connection. She pictured a dry-erase board at the police station. Plainclothes cops staring at the dotted line connecting the note in the book to Nina. And Nina to Sam Wood's death. She was a dotted line away from being hauled in for questioning.

Pedal to the floor, she veered off the highway. The car practically drove itself to Larimer Square downtown. She drove around the square. The brick buildings, asleep for years, usually came alive like paintings, somehow quieting tension inside her. She hooked right, down a tree-lined street. None of it seemed to help.

She cruised by The Galleries, considered parking, wandering the labyrinth of shops. In the end, she popped into Pie-pie for a hot tea to go. Piper owned Pie-pie. From Nina's first visit, she had been drawn to Piper's quiet nature. Nina yearned for her kind eyes. The way she glided through the restaurant, offering all of herself to her customers, soaking in every word, yet effortless. Nina needed the familiarity to shake off the feeling of drowning.

But she couldn't. The clues somehow led to her involvement. The note, the initials. And the odd sensations. Nina intended to slide back into the car and head toward her condo, her original destination. After a few miles, she found herself driving to the church. Nervously, she eyed the passenger seat where the book rested. Its weight caused the seat belt warning light to flash on and off. She had an urge to pull over and examine the note again. Everything about the note bothered her. The part about her father not having talent. The possibility that Sam Wood had written the note.

It was Wednesday. The same day last week when Jack had rescued her from the reporter. She followed the length of the church building, to the rise of manicured grass where gravestones stood like rows of dominoes. The sky above a weak tea stain, making the day dreary and somber.

She found Jack sitting under the pergola. "I expected to find you inside filling the hot tub."

He glanced up from his laptop. "Nina." He smiled. "You've come to be baptized?"

"I can't claim I'm here for an eye exam." The book dangled precariously by her side. She couldn't shake the finger-burning thing, and although she didn't feel that now, she wasn't taking any chances. She glanced back at the car. "Honestly, the car just drove here."

"Really?" He chuckled. "Self-driving cars. You'll have to take me for a spin sometime."

She smiled, though it wasn't a real smile. Her thoughts were on the note. Jack was a reasonable man. She wanted his take. She found him approachable. Doctors, after all, were good listeners. At least he was.

Jack's gaze fell to the book. "By the picture on the cover, I'm guessing that's not a bible?"

"An art book." She tried to hide her concern. "The one we talked about."

"You found it." He scratched his chin. "No paint-by-number pictures?" He closed the laptop, set it beside him on the bench. "Let's have a look."

She hesitated. "It's not so much the book." She made a face. "It's what I found on the last page." But it was also the book. The creepy sensations. All of it leaving her on edge.

Carefully, she opened the spine, flipped to the last page, and held the book up so he could read the note.

"A cocky fellow." His eyes brightened. "Or maybe a woman?"

She hadn't considered SW could be a woman. She had only considered Sam Wood.

"After what you told me about your father, I'm guessing you're the she?"

Nina plunked down beside him. "The thing is, my dad was a beautiful painter. I hate to think he was discouraged by an offhanded note." She reread the note, then looked up at Jack. "I'm stuck on the initials. SW has to be Sam Wood. There's a closer connection now between the two of us." She was staring up at Jack, waiting for a dose of his sound advice. A reasonable explanation that would take away the dark cloud she had felt like she had been under since she had read the note.

He ruffled his hair. "Could be, I guess." He stripped the note from the book, and Nina braced herself, expecting Jack to feel something like she had.

Nothing happened. He examined the other side of the sticky note. "Do you recall your parents' friends? Anyone with these initials?"

She couldn't think of anyone. "Kids don't usually know adult first names. It's Mr. This and Mrs. That. Besides, my parents didn't have many friends. At least not that I knew."

"Maybe it's a joke," Jack offered, but it didn't seem like a joke.

"After everything, I can't believe that's your comment." She closed the book. Had she worked herself up for no reason? No. The note wasn't a joke.

"Do you have any of his paintings?" Jack shifted toward the laptop and began stuffing it into a leather pouch. "I'm curious about this giant of a man with serious talent."

"No." Nina stood. "But I know where to find one." Maybe she'd find a clue to SW at her father's condo. It was long past time to clear out the rest of his belongings. She'd stalled, thinking one day he would come home.

She fished out the car keys from her pocket. She gathered the book, forgetting all about the bad mojo. With a purposeful pause, she stared into his eyes. "I need you to believe me."

"I do." He looked up, seeming surprised she would think that.

She shoved a chunk of hair behind her ear. "My life is on the line. I'm certain Kanoy has some plainclothes guy tailing me. Waiting."

They shifted back toward the parking lot, scanning cars and the handful of people strolling to or from the church, searching for anyone suspicious.

A man sat inside a silver Lincoln parked in the first row. In the faint light, she couldn't make out the man's features. As if he realized they were watching, the hum of an engine revved. He backed out of the space and slipped away.

# 1985

# SIXTEEN

That first trip with Skylar to deliver books which ended at Cyrus's house changed Sam's life. Beyond minor kid pranks, like stealing candy bars and bubble gum, Sam had now stolen a collector's book from the schmuck at Cassini's. What came next still boggles his mind.

Sam's fascination with Cyrus began the moment Cyrus ushered Sam and Skylar inside the modest two-story. Heavy lamps with low-watt bulbs diffused the light, making the room appear hazy. The furnishings were practical and well worn. A family lived there. A real home, not like the upscale hotel vibe at his parents' house.

"Come, come." Cyrus motioned, and they followed him across the patterned rug, navigating a barrel chair to the edge of a wooden coffee table, marred and stained.

Cyrus perched beside the fireplace, resting a foot on the raised hearth. Retrieving a pipe from his pocket, he tapped it against the mantel's underbelly, depositing a dust of tobacco into the fire. He wore glasses and a worn sweater frayed at the cuffs. Thinning, brackish hair above his ears appeared disheveled. And he wore Hush Puppies. No one wore Hush Puppies anymore.

Sam looked around. Every space held a trinket. Nothing that appeared expensive. Memory pieces, he gathered. A delicate vase. A statue of a Greek god or something like that. A jeweled butterfly sat on an ornately carved box. Stained glass depicting trees, one bright and cheerful, the other barren and stark. Pungent leather and sweet spices tickled his nose. And mint. Yes, he could almost taste the menthol trickling down his throat.

"I'm quite proud of my latest, Skylar," Cyrus gestured with the tilt of his head and meandered down the hall. "I'm finding my stride. Creating one-of-a-kind pieces."

Skylar followed on his heels. Sam, lost in the allure of a toss-your-socks-on-the-floor-and-curl-up-in-front-of-the-fire room, caught up just as Cyrus lifted a bedsheet off a canvas. A bit theatrical for Sam's taste.

"Another painting." Skylar's voice trilled. She turned to Sam, excitement lighting her eyes.

The easel held a rather dull painting. At least, Sam saw it that way. Then again, he didn't know much about painting other than a class or two in college.

"Cream on white?" Skylar asked. She tucked the books she'd brought beneath her arm and clapped.

Cyrus stepped closer, slipped his hands into the pockets of his trousers, and admired the canvas with a critical eye. "I see much more."

"Like what?" Sam said, arms crossed. He struggled to see anything beyond blotches. Certainly, he could paint better than that monstrosity.

"Look, Sam." Skylar stepped closer and pointed to a creamy blob. She shifted to Cyrus. "A building?" she asked with a measure of uncertainty.

The excitement on Cyrus's face waned.

"A bench, maybe?" she offered.

Ridiculous. She was guessing, no different than charades.

"Yes." The older man's eyes widened. "A bench outside Paris." With a bony finger, he pointed out the faint, pointy shape to the left rising skyward. "The Eiffel Tower." He retrieved the pipe from his pocket, cradled the bowl as if he planned to light up in celebration. For an old guy, he didn't have much of a chest, but it puffed like a bird.

"The clouds were low that day," Cyrus began. "Still, the city was alive. Cheese wafting from the fromager. Warm bread baking at the patisserie around the corner. The sky hung low over the city; a volt of excitement danced in the air."

A smile broke wide across Skylar's face as if his words brought intoxicating images so real, it seemed she could smell the damned food.

"So." Sam dipped his head to view the painting from another angle. "A bench." He paused. "Huh." He crossed his arms. "Wow." "Wow" was his go-to response when nothing positive came to mind, yet something was expected.

Cyrus sighed. Ignoring Sam altogether, he shifted to Skylar. "Now, about those books. I hope Martha found both editions?" His eyes trailed to the package Skylar held against her chest.

"She did." Skylar handed him the books. She said to Sam, "Cyrus has traveled the world. In fact, he met his wife in Marrakesh."

"Though she's from Colorado," Cyrus corrected. "A séance prompted her excursion. She claims a spirit brought us together." He flailed his arms, a botched attempt to appear ghostly. Seemingly uncomfortable with his display, he hugged himself. "I'll leave it to the Greek gods. Opposites attract, they say. And let's not forget about the allure of romance on foreign soil."

"I can't imagine Marrakesh." Skylar gazed back at the painting, her cheeks aglow. "Or Paris."

"Not extravagant adventures," Cyrus reminded her. "Hostels, university rooms. I traveled on the cheap."

Skylar's draw to this man was obvious. The moment she had stepped inside, she'd entered another world. And Cyrus was her private escort.

"I traveled to India." Sam rocked back on his heels. "Rode an elephant, in fact."

Skylar's smile faded. Either India didn't interest her, or she'd seen through his one-upmanship.

"I've taken students abroad." Cyrus picked up the bedsheet and carefully draped it back over the painting. "Elephants, I found, were gentle beasts."

Sam didn't remember it that way. Then again, he had been six and terrified. "So you teach?" He was curious to know more about this man who'd captured Skylar's attention.

"He used to," Skylar explained, leaving Cyrus with his mouth open. "Now he buys and sells books."

"Not much selling. Painting has captured my interest." His unruly brows lifted.

"I can see that," Sam said smugly.

Outside, Sam sank heavily in the car seat. He looked at Skylar. "You really think that guy can paint? Maybe he should stick to buying books."

Skylar frowned. "It's not about that. He's a Renaissance man, and I enjoy hearing about his life." She tucked her purse on the floorboard. "Where could I possibly experience anything remotely sophisticated in Broadmoor?"

"Nowhere," Sam said flatly. He gripped the steering wheel. It occurred to him that he could give her that world and more. If. And it was a big if. If he made peace with his father.

"Skylar," he said softly. A flicker of moonlight caught her hoop earring. Leaning in, he brushed her lips with his. Surprise brightened her cheeks. He looked away, cleared his throat, and started the car.

On the ride back to Donovan's, they remained silent; their goodbyes robotic, neither knowing what to say or do. As he watched the headlights on her Beetle swerve out of Donovan's parking lot, he already missed the hint of vanilla he'd tasted on her lips. Oddly, his thoughts drifted to Cyrus. Girls came and went. But something about him intrigued Sam. Maybe it was his eccentric ways, his unique finds displayed in that pillbox house. A piece of clutter holding a story or two.

But it was something else. Something *about* Cyrus.

For sure, it wasn't his ability to paint.

# SEVENTEEN

Sam's father would say Sam didn't think things through. Maybe that was true. Sam liked not knowing what was coming around the bend.

The edges of something brilliant was forming. The cerebral giddiness kept Sam alert. He couldn't see it yet, but he knew it had to do with Cyrus.

When Sam played chauffeur again, a pricey pipe tobacco tin was stowed in the glove box. As before, Skylar left Cyrus's stop until the last. The visit, however, ended abruptly.

"My Nina's come down with a sore throat," Cyrus said after opening the door. "Her mother is clearing Mrs. Zint next door of evil spirits. That's what I'm told. And I need not hear more." He waved a hand in the air. "It's all hooey," he groused. "Regardless, I'm happily a nursemaid tonight to my Nina." Smile lines creased each side of his face.

Skylar handed over the delivery. "*Who Stole the Bird's Nest?* Call with any new titles, and Martha will work her magic."

"Magic, indeed."

Skylar and Sam were standing on the porch outside the door. The moon was full, the mosquitos hungry. Sam slapped his neck. Irritation lingered on his face as Skylar said her goodbyes.

Sam shook the man's hand. "I came across this." He retrieved the can from his pocket. "Thought you might enjoy it."

Cyrus's forehead creased. He glanced at Sam. "You don't look like a pipe man." Cyrus took the can, held it at arm's length to read the label in the light provided by a wall lantern, chipped and rusty.

"No," Sam admitted.

An odd look befell Cyrus's angular face. He was waiting for an explanation. Of course there was one. Sam wanted something from Cyrus. What, he wasn't sure. Cyrus, a clear contradiction of Sam's father, intrigued Sam. Maybe that was where the interest ended. Pure curiosity in a gentle soul who seemed to have all he wanted. A man who looked at Sam with genuine interest, as if Sam had something interesting to say. Which made Sam all the more fascinated to be in his presence.

"Good night, then," Sam stepped backward and bowed his head before returning to the car.

───────

Inside the trailer, the crackle of tree limbs bending to the wind awakened Sam. Perspiration dampened his pillow. He flipped the pillow and closed his eyes.

Dreams of his father kept surfacing. Tired, familiar conversations circled Sam's dream. Him and his father. *Damn it, son. Say the word, and you're back in the fold.* Which meant, of course, working corporate hours at the investment firm, a sweet salary, and a constant reminder of what a disappointment Edward Wood III's boy was and still is.

Waltrip, Wood, and Sons, a three-story steel marvel camped on the outskirts of Broadmoor's tourist district. The monstrosity of metal proved to be a constant reminder of Sam's worthless existence. Waltrip had ponied up two golden boys. The sign should have read *Waltrip and Sons and Wood.* Some families have black sheep. Sam was more a feral horse roaming free and wild. No matter what Sam did, from striking out at Little League to choosing liberal arts over economics at college and a thousand other profound moments, he could never please his father.

Sam switched onto his back, sloughed off the heavy blanket. Giving up on sleep, he slid out of bed and tapped on the light above the compact kitchen. In the drawer beneath the bed, Sam rifled through notebooks from college he should have tossed long ago. Yet here he was, thumbing through syllabuses and books looking for his pen-and-ink drawings. He found the folder and flipped through the drawings: one tennis shoe, a bike lock, Pikes Peak.

A low groan of thunder rumbled. Sam froze. The tiny trailer warbled before lightning hit, illuminating the pages. Sam grinned down at his drawings. They weren't half-bad. Or was he an egoist cut from the same cloth as his father? He shuffled through the pictures, remembering his father doing the same. "Child's play." He had eyeballed Sam. "Good coin's waiting, Sam. Damned good coin."

His father had shoved the pad across the table, over the edge, onto the cement. They were sitting in the quad at Regis University, his father in a stiff suit and tie; Sam, a ball cap and jeans. He locked angry eyes on his father, holding in a rash of swear words, aware of his drawing pressed against the gritty cement.

Now Sam unfolded those pages, a casualty from the fall. Rooting through the drawer for a blank sheet of paper, he grabbed a pencil and began making a list of the supplies he would need to paint.

In oil, like Cyrus.

# EIGHTEEN

Despite blinding rain, Sam navigated the roads to Cyrus's bungalow. The scent of kindled wood welcomed him, along with a firm handshake.

"It's early for a beer." Cyrus considered Sam with a furrowed brow as he stepped inside and shed his bulky overcoat.

"Soda's fine." Sam moved to the fireplace, rubbed his hands together. "The wife around?" he asked over his shoulder.

"A gem fair." Cyrus returned with a bubbly glass and handed it to Sam. A long look followed, Cyrus probably wondering why Sam had stopped by unannounced.

"How's your daughter? Nina, is it?" Sam sunk into the sofa, making himself at home.

"In her room. We just finished building a fort." He shrugged. "She calls it her castle."

"Kids," Sam rolled his eyes. He'd never built a fort in his room. Then again, he hadn't grown up like most kids.

The fire crackled. Sam gulped down the root beer, thinking about how he could bring up the paintings in his trunk. Two rudimentary landscapes from books he had borrowed from the bookstore. He was no Renoir, but they weren't half-bad. At least, Sam thought so.

Cyrus folded into the barrel chair, crossed his narrow legs, exposing brown-and-gold argyle socks.

"I've taken up the brush," Sam began. "Haven't gotten my bearings yet." He waited for a reaction. He wanted one, and Cyrus delivered with an enthusiastic nod.

"Bravo, Sam." Cyrus grew serious. "I paint for Nina. She marvels at the canvas. When I show her Picasso, Rembrandt, her tiny fingers trace the glossy photos. At four, she could hold a brush. Steady as a surgeon." He grinned widely and pulled in an expansive breath. "She thinks my stick figures are masterpieces."

"And *Paris Bench*?" Sam eased into the soft cushions, stretched his back against the busy pattern.

"Belongs in the Louvre." Cyrus chuckled. "Well, she doesn't know the Louvre, but Daddy's hallway will do."

Cyrus's painting now made sense. For the love of a child. Sam sat with that, took in the fire, and tried to imagine what that kind of love felt like. The fire danced, and for a moment, he felt a loss, missing something he had never had. He'd never been a talker, but something in the way Cyrus perched in the chair, hands folded and attentive, eased Sam.

He shifted to Cyrus. Slowly, thoughtfully, he began talking. And Cyrus listened. Their childhoods weren't similar, but both had been whisked off to boarding schools too young and rarely brought home. Sam emptied himself of memories of his father without expectation. Cyrus didn't say much. He didn't have to. His kind eyes glistened. He nodded here and there and sat attentively, one hand over the other, listening completely.

With his father, Sam was always waiting for a barrage of disparaging remarks. His voice freed from a deep place inside where he always held his tongue, knowing his voice didn't matter.

Talk drifted into travel, digressed to food and, eventually, sports.

"No, never been to a ball game," Cyrus admitted.

"Cricket, then?" Sam was on his second glass of root beer.

"Golf." Cyrus held up a finger. "Watched. Not played."

The banter continued. Sam hefted another log on the fire.

Cyrus, glancing at the flames, seemed lost in thought. The glow reflected on his rather pale skin. Sam figured he'd stayed long enough. It was time to go. But something kept him lingering beside the fireplace, sharing the rainy afternoon in a comfortable home with a man who made time for Sam, who treated him fairly, without ridicule or arrogance.

"I should check on Nina." Cyrus rose and crept up the stairs.

Sam warmed his hands. He glanced up the staircase. The creak of heavy footsteps above confirmed Cyrus's location overhead. Murmured voices followed.

Sam wanted to see the painting. A quick peek. He glanced back at the stairway before stepping into the alcove where the painting stood, naked and lifeless.

In front of the painting, Sam rubbed his forehead. It looked too modern, too unrealistic, experimental in shape and form. Poorly painted for sure. It didn't look like the type of painting Cyrus would paint.

In the daylight, the easel caught light from the window despite the passing clouds. Sam moved closer. Now in the twilight of the cloudy afternoon, the layers of paint on *Paris Bench* glistened like the tips of churning waves. The phenomena, though mildly interesting, didn't change Sam's view of the painting. He ran a thumb over the jagged slope of land, the layer of color no different than the sky. Blobs. Formations of creamy blobs.

His gaze drifted to the table beside the painting. A book laid open to a painting exactly like the one on the easel. Sam blinked. His eyes darted back and forth between the two paintings.

He flipped to the cover, careful not to disturb the placement of the book. *Forgotten Masters.* Sam was certain the book wasn't on the table last time. Clever, really. Buying collectible books and tossing in a few art books to copy from. Was he a forger or copying a master for pleasure? Either way Cyrus had lied. This wasn't his painting.

Sam ran a hand down his face and breathed a heavy sigh. Why was Cyrus claiming he had painted it? People copied paintings all the time but made that fact common knowledge. Was he seeking recognition? Was he planning on selling it? It wasn't exactly forgery, yet Cyrus had made it sound like the painting was his creation. Disappointment washed over Sam. He really liked Cyrus. Mostly, he liked the way Cyrus treated him.

Sam glanced around the room. His perfect image of Cyrus had splintered. Even good guys had a smidgen of bad in them, he reasoned. He winced, thinking of Cyrus's story about the sights and smells in Paris. What a crock. Sam had grown tired of being disappointed. In his father. Now Cyrus. Sam wanted to pummel the canvas. Hands fisted, he fought the urge.

Instead, he did something worse.

# NINETEEN

The book had replaced the coveted spot where Tisha had placed the amethyst on the nightstand beside the bed.

Having not seen the book for years, sweet memories of her father whispered to Nina in the night, nudging her to dive inside and find hidden jewels. Bright stories woven with silliness. And oodles of sloppy paint.

During the day, roaming from one room to another, she would pass the guest room, and her senses would heighten as if the book were calling her. Eventually, she would give in, hike onto the bed, and escape among the scribbles and watery smudges. The book held goodness. She tried to ignore any thoughts about the note or the uneasiness that taunted her at times, when she allowed herself to remember the tingling in her fingers, the feeling something was off. She would close it purposely before she reached the last page. Still bracing for the brief jolt. Pretending the note wasn't there, keeping the book as she remembered it. Simply playful times with her father.

Whenever she left the house, the book traveled with her. She wouldn't put it past her mother to delve into her private memories.

An offhanded remark about her father often crept into Tisha's memories. Nina didn't find her sarcasm the least bit amusing.

She'd put off going to her father's condo. Any chore to distract her. This morning, she was headed to The Fishing Hole, as she liked to call Jack's back office. She reached for the book and paused. She considered the cover. A cheery yellow vase, a tranquil wash of sky surrounding it. How could something so beautiful have such a hold on her? Snatching the book, she slipped out the front door.

Detective Kanoy was standing beside her car.

"I don't have time today to chat," she said, walking briskly past him and opening the car door.

His squinting eyes lit with a twinkle of mischief as if this intrusion was a game to him. "We tail suspects, Ms. Shubert. A simple police tactic. Even you should know that."

"You should look harder for someone else." She slung the seat belt across her chest, clicked in, and started the car, unwilling to grace him with her attention. When she reached for the door handle, he clutched the doorframe, stopping her.

"We're close." His gaze flicked off her to the passenger seat. "What do we have there?"

Nina honked the horn, startling him. He recoiled from the car. Nina shut the door and sped off.

———————

The bottom dweller's serpentine scales caught light from the open blinds, giving him a deep-indigo glow. "Bob Dylan looks happy." She turned to Jack. He was bending over a bowl, slurping ramen at his makeshift table and chairs in his back office.

"I'm happy to say I haven't forgotten to feed him this week."

Nina set the book on the counter and joined Jack. He didn't disappoint. He'd brought the wontons she'd requested. She plucked one and dipped it in soy sauce. "What about a love interest for Bob?" She licked her finger, glanced back at the tank.

"Does the name have to have the same initials as Bottom Dweller?"

"That depends." She took another bite. "All fish are bottom dwellers, aren't they?"

"Not sure."

"I like the initial theme." She sipped her soda. "How about we use Fishing Hole? FH."

Jack's head bobbled as he considered the idea. "Florence Henderson?"

"I think Bob would rather have Faith Hill in the tank with him." Nina's eyes flickered.

"Agreed." Jack snuck a wonton off Nina's plate, and she pretended to be irritated.

"I'm going to my dad's condo to pick up *Paris Bench*." Nina gobbled the last bite, squished the foil into a ball, and tossed it in the bag. "Same time Friday?" She rose and went to the counter to grab her traveling companion, the book.

"If you pick out Faith." She turned to face Jack. "I'll treat."

Jack's eyes fell to the floor, and hers followed. The yellow sticky note from the back page of the book had fluttered to the carpet. Nina bent down. She didn't want to look at it and snatched it up, tucked it in her pocket.

"Did you check at your father's for any clues to who SW could be?"

"I haven't had time," she lied and gathered up their plates, tossed them in the trash. "I'll do that today."

"I think you'd feel better getting to the bottom of this."

She didn't want to listen. He was right, she knew. But if SW was Sam Wood . . . She shuddered.

"Wherever this leads, it's time to figure it out." He paused. He was watching her poke through her purse on the counter, ignoring him. "Your father must have had an address book or place he kept his contacts."

Hearing him speak in the past tense about her father drew her back. Nina felt guilty for not telling Jack the truth about him. She would at some point. Just not now. "I have his phone," she offered. "He used it to call me or his buddy Joe. I doubt he had many other contacts." Nina had never considered her father having a social life. He didn't talk about friends. In a way, she had been his world. Should she have misgivings about that?

Her thoughts drifted to his condo, a blank canvas compared with their home in Broadmoor. He had tossed out many of his tchotchkes and sold what valuables had remained, only moving the necessities. One thing, though, had followed him to Colorado Springs: his messy desk. "My dad had one of those circular things with index card thingamajigs that you turn." She used her hands to paint a picture.

"A Rolodex? I thought those things were outlawed." Jack sucked down the last of his water bottle. "I'd rifle through it for possible names." He shrugged. "It's worth a try."

─────────

The condo was dark, the air stale. Nina flung open the blackout drapes. Dust particles glistened in the light. Ugh.

She waved a hand in the air as she walked to the back door and shoved open the slider. Fresh air bellowed in. Pleased, Nina traipsed up the stairs to her father's study.

Jack had been right. Clunky and archaic, the Rolodex barely turned. It contained a dozen or so cards. Nina frowned, folded into the chair, and slid the contraption front and center. The wheel clacked along as she turned it to find the *W* tab, which was actually *V–Z*. She flipped through the three cards there.

*Wahoo Taco.* Obviously a restaurant by the smudge of red sauce that stained the card.

*Robert Wilson.* Below was written *Toyota dealership* in her father's neat penmanship.

*Stuart Warner.* Nothing else but a phone number.

She chewed on the inside of her cheek, considering the card with Stuart Warner's name. There were no other cards in the *W* section. She hunted through all the letters in case Sam's card was misplaced. She sighed. No card with Sam Wood's name on it.

She let out a breath and flopped back in the chair, not sure if she was pleased or disappointed. Nina plucked the card with Stuart Warner's information. SW. *He could be the one who wrote the note.* Reaching for her phone, she called him.

⬤——⬤

It seemed surreal meeting Stuart, the man who had possibly penned the note so many years ago. A man who theoretically claimed to know her. *She's better than you, Cy. Talent skips a generation. Don't I know. Focus on her. SW*

Then again, he could be a guy who happened to share the same initials.

Stuart Warner seemed a nice-enough man on the phone and agreed to meet Nina at his work at 4:00 p.m. Nina stood outside Lumber Emporium cradling the book, working up the nerve to go inside. Lumber Emporium appeared a tad homier than a big-box store. Wooden carved black bears holding silly signs and fall foliage welcomed patrons at the entrance. It didn't seem like a place where a killer worked. *Neither did an art gallery,* she reminded herself. Sucking in a breath, she strolled inside.

A husky man in jeans and a flannel shirt glanced in her direction before sauntering over. Older, sixtyish, he wore a knitted cap with earflaps and a warm smile. He looked like his voice. Kind. The earflaps seemed a bit childish and odd for a man his age. Still, Nina immediately felt silly for coming.

"Nina?" He motioned her away from the entrance, where customers shuffled by with flat carts stacked with lumber. "You're Cyrus's daughter?" He frowned as if he had no idea who her father was.

Nina nodded. "I found your name in his files. I was curious how you knew him." She tried to sound matter-of-fact. She didn't want to upset him. If he was the one who had written the note, she had a slew of questions and wanted his cooperation.

His eyes dropped to the book before returning to the question, making Nina suspicious. She shifted the book to the other arm to see if his eyes followed. They didn't.

"Honestly, I didn't know your dad. When you called, I racked my brain." He chuckled deep in his chest. "A ton of old folks pop in for advice on projects around the house." Stuart scratched the side of his whiskered face. "Can't say I remember all their names and faces."

"Most people don't have store employees' personal phone numbers." Tightening her grip on the book, she faked a smile. She realized she sounded like Kanoy, and that wasn't her intention.

Stuart glanced over his shoulder. He appeared nervous and stepped closer, whispering, "I freelance here and there. Maybe I helped your father with a project." He winked.

Seemed plausible. Nina knew her father hadn't been handy around the house. Relief came along with disappointment. Most likely he wasn't the one. Still. She flipped the book around and opened it to the last page. "Did you write this note?"

He squinted and swiped a hand across his eyes before patting the pockets of his flannel. The way his broad shoulders hunched and his chin doubled over and rested on his chest sparked a memory. From where or when, she didn't remember.

"Must have left my readers at home."

Nina's gaze quickly traveled to his. She nodded, giving him ample time to give the note another look. He cleared his throat, tried again. "My writing isn't near as neat. Mine's barely legible."

That wasn't an answer. She snapped the book closed and smiled tightly. That should have been the end of it, but she plugged on. "Do you know," she began, then caught herself. "Did you know Sam Wood?"

Stuart shook his head. "No, ma'am." He shoved a hand in the pocket of his apron, pulled out a tape measure, and fiddled with it. "Tell your father hello for me. I'd be happy to help him out again legit-like. It's my last month here." He wrestled a finger underneath an earflap and poked a knuckle in his ear. "Vertigo," he explained.

Nina wrestled with what she had just seen. She was staring at the cap, the red cap and, specifically, the silly flaps. She jerked away, retrained her eyes on Stuart's face. "You're retiring?"

"Drive's too far. I relocated to Manitou Springs months ago. A few blocks north of the Caspian Hotel and The Galleries."

Dawning came in a sudden inhale. *The sad man at the other end of the bar at the Caspian, thumping the bar top.* Her gaze drifted to his pudgy hands. *Thick fingers thumping the countertop.* Then up to the red cap. Just like the man in the bar, except his was pulled low, covering his forehead. Had that hat had flaps? Her hand suddenly shot to her lips. She pretended to have hiccupped and let out a nervous chuckle. Their eyes met. Had he realized she knew who he was?

"Ma'am, are you all right?"

Her cheeks must have flushed. Nina tried to find a brittle smile. No words escaped her lips. She just nodded. With the book against her chest, she hightailed it to the car as fast as her Skechers would travel. Inside the Prius, breathless and frazzled, she called Jack.

"It's him. Stuart killed Sam." She was panting, eyes darting between the windshield, the rearview mirror, and the side mirror, expecting Stuart to appear. With a shaky hand, she started the car and locked the doors.

"Wow. Slow down. What happened?"

With feathered breaths, she told Jack. Once the details were laid out, her breathing had slowed. A measure of sense returned, and she no longer felt agitated.

"That's a big jump: the book somehow being related to Sam's death." Jack paused. "I don't see it."

She shifted the phone to her other ear. She'd been pressing it too closely, causing her earring to loosen. "I just know. I can't explain it. They're related, Jack."

He paused. "Listen, you want me to pick you up? We could get your car later."

*He's worried about me and my damned car instead of Stuart Warner. A man who slandered my dad and somehow knows me.* Had Jack listened to anything she had said?

"It's a big leap, Nina." Jack sighed. "Are you certain it was him at the bar in the Caspian?"

It was true. She had never really seen the sad man's face. And she wasn't sure about the knitted cap. Did it have earflaps? And even if it had, they were in snow country. Everyone wore those silly caps.

"No. You're right." She buried her face in her hands. She didn't trust herself. "The thing is everyone looks suspicious," she admitted. A part of her wanted Stuart to be guilty of something. Anything to get Kanoy off her back and end this nightmare. "I should tell Kanoy."

"Unless you have hard evidence, Nina, he'll think you're tossing out scenarios to get him off your case."

Her thoughts buzzed. She had to dig deeper into Stuart.

# TWENTY

With *Paris Bench* settled in the back seat of her Prius, Nina breezed along a familiar route she traveled from her father's condo three blocks from The Art Loft at The Galleries.

Her thoughts on her encounter with Stuart, she missed her turnoff and continued along the road that eventually circled The Galleries. The lush, tropical landscape and rustic yet modern buildings drew people, even if only for a walk along the winding paths or raised-slat boardwalks snaking toward another level, deeper inside the labyrinth of shops.

Nina slowed as she approached a rise of Bermuda grass between buildings. The display window of The Art Loft winked in the distance. Track lighting illuminated the window, the feature painting—this month, a playful oil by Sally K. Abstract, vibrant flowers gracing a woman's head. Nina remembered the large canvas coming in. The delicious unveiling of a new painting always brought excitement. Whatever the medium and form, it brought life to the gallery and a heightened sense of her role in the scheme of things: to not only show off the sparkly, new toy but also remind her she was a painter, a creator of shiny and beautiful art too.

Nina pulled to the curb. She missed The Art Loft. She missed being surrounded by art. Often, the gallery was hers alone, especially when she had the opening shift. Before she would switch on a smooth-jazz CD, she would walk the gallery, weaving her way through each vignette. Every painting lit up like a star, waiting to be seen. That private time reminded her of the hours she had admired *Paris Bench*. Well, maybe not hours, but to a kid, it had seemed that way. Her private star created just for her.

Nina spotted Stacey—her gait a fast walk with a slight bounce—parade past the window. Nina couldn't help herself. She popped out of the car, crossed the street, and wound her way along the path to The Art Loft.

Inside, familiar smells tickled her nose: varnish, citrus, pine from hand-stretched canvases. Exposed pipes snaked through the shop, creating its own rather industrial art. Nina strolled past the feature piece near the front entrance. A few of her favorites still hung like familiar friends. A creaking sound, followed by a grunt, sounded from the back of the gallery. Nina found Stacey balancing on a ladder, struggling to hang a bulky painting.

"Let me help with that." Nina dropped her purse at the counter. Standing between the ladder and bracing against the wall, she supported the canvas and heaved upward. The tag-team effort eased the painting onto the hook.

"Voilà." Nina scooted away from the wall, gave a thumbs-up.

Stacey climbed off the ladder. "We miss you here."

Nina didn't expect a hug. A warm smile would have been nice. "I miss being here." *I miss my Winsor & Newton palette. I miss my brushes. I even miss my speckled water can.*

Both glanced up at the trio of paintings. Art deco lollipops in watercolor. "I thought real lollipops would be a nice touch." Stacey plucked a handful from her puffy vest. "Thought I'd set out a glass bowl of each color. Something for customers to suck on while the paintings suck them in. Ha!" Without skipping a beat, she popped a sucker in her mouth and clumped to the back room with the ladder in tow.

Nina continued walking the gallery, a solemn stroll, seeing what had sold, what remained. She thought of *Paris Bench* on display here. It deserved to be a shining star for everyone to see. No. *Paris Bench* was her childhood. Not to be shared. Besides, consignment pieces were here to be sold. Not happening.

Squeaky rubber soles announced Stacey, carrying a stack of printer paper. "Any news on the case?" In other words, *Have you been cleared?*

Nina frowned. "Not on my end. You? Reporters still coming by?"

"Less often." Stacey fiddled with the edge of the middle painting, adjusting it a smidgeon. She set the stack of papers on the desk. Background information on the artist of the lollipop collection. "I called the police."

"Why?" Nina frowned again. "What did they say?"

"Nothing." Stacey dropped into a chair. She swiveled toward Nina and removed the sucker. "Are you hanging in there?"

Nina let out a breath. "As well as I can." She rested on the edge of the desk, played with the pens and pencils in one of Tanya Keith's Sgraffito Design mugs. She had showed there last winter, and Stacey had bought a few pieces. Apparently, this week, she was using one of the mugs to hold her pens. "I picked up a piece of my dad's art today." Nina brightened. "I'm excited to hang it up, bring a piece of him home." Stacey didn't know her father's story. No one did.

"I'd love to see it."

"Really?" Nina was surprised. Stacey kept things professional, but then, this was art. Her baby.

Nina looked away, considered the idea. "Okay," she said slowly and carefully. She wanted to add a list of caveats. Stacey could be cruel at times. Art was subjective, but Nina knew *Paris Bench* was good. Damned good. "I'll bring it in."

Nina carefully laid the painting on the desk. She stepped back, admiring the creamy textures, the pronounced shadow definitions, the Eiffel Tower soaring into the muddy sky. "He hid this gem." Nina smiled. Her father had never said much about the painting. For that, she admired his humility on top of his talent. "I guess he didn't care if anyone else saw it."

Stacey stepped closer. "Do you mind?"

Nina shook her head.

"He painted in oils." It wasn't a question, though lines formed between Stacey's perfectly plucked brows. "The way you spoke about your dad, I thought you shared the same medium."

She never really thought about why she had chosen watercolor. "Oils are definitely easier," Nina responded. "At least, that's what you read. And changing colors and shapes are a snap." She followed the angular line of the Eiffel Tower, perfectly symmetrical. "Fixing line work with oils is a no-brainer. Try and try again until you get it right."

Watercolor, she'd learned, didn't offer that grace. Some didn't agree and said that, given the highest-quality paper and a good scrubbing, watercolor could, in theory, disappear. That experience eluded Nina. Water had a mind of its own. Although she had to admit it often created unexpected beauty that took years to achieve. Nina liked that it was hard. Maybe that was who she was. Always pushing toward something. A higher award. Better technique. Selling paintings.

Stacey lifted the edge of the frame. She held the canvas at an angle. "Huh. It's not signed."

"Isn't it?" Nina scoured the right corner.

"Do you mind if I touch it?"

Nine shrugged. "Go ahead."

Stacey's finger grazed over the painted surface. "See this?" She pointed to a change in color in the foreground creating a rise beside the bench. "It's a different shade. Almost looks like someone painted over this spot. And I see other spots too."

"I doubt it means anything." Nina dismissed the idea with a shrug. "My dad was eccentric. Who knows what technique he was using."

"Do you mind if I take a picture? Something's not right." Stacey frowned. "I can't flesh it out just yet." Chewing her lip, she reached across the desk for her phone.

Nina spoke abruptly. "No picture." She confiscated the painting, held it against her chest away from Stacey's curious gaze. "There's been enough upheaval in my life lately. It's best if I take *Paris Bench* home."

There was a beat of silence: Nina holding the painting, Stacey staring, waiting. Nina smiled. "Thanks, though, for your interest. I'm sure it's nothing." She hoped she hadn't offended Stacey or jeopardized her chances of returning to work.

———

Nina wasted no time removing *The Kiss* above her desk. With a firm grasp and upward motion, she unhooked the painting.

*Paris Bench* rested on the desk, its back side facing up. Nina tested the braided wire hanging the length of the canvas. Her father had the painting professionally framed. A once-sturdy manila paper covered the back. Now brittle, the paper had torn near the top.

Nina reached for the tape on the desk and tore off a strip. She played with the edges of the manila paper to draw the edges together. It was tough with sticky tape dangling from her fingers and maneuvering her hands over the artwork.

The painting slipped. Thank God she caught it before it hit the tile floor. Her breath hitched. She swallowed hard when she noticed the paper had ripped, exposing a good part of the back side of the canvas.

*Damn.*

Affixed to the bottom corner of the canvas, a worn and peeling sticker from Westham's Framing and Art drew her attention. Nina sidled to the other end of the canvas for a better look. The sticker listed the painting's owner and the date the painting would be ready for pick up.

Nina never read the date. She was staring at the name of the owner: *Sam Wood.*

# TWENTY-ONE

*Sam Wood?*

Nina tore at the rest of the brittle paper, looking for any-thing that would explain why *his* name was on her father's painting. She found nothing. She rubbed the back of her neck. A sharp smell hit her. Masculine and energetic yet jarring.

Nina stepped away from the painting. The odor dissipated.

Cautiously, she approached *Paris Bench*, eyes fixed on the can-vas. Bracing herself, she breathed in. To her surprise, the smell had vanished.

She splayed a hand above the painting. Did she dare touch it again? She thought of her mother's fingertips tracing signatures in the guest book at the memorial. Were the sensations and smells Nina experienced similar to Tisha's? Nina never considered she had the gift because she didn't believe in it.

Holding her breath, she touched the smooth edge of the frame, braced for a reaction, but there was none. Gingerly, she carried the canvas into the living room, where the vaulted ceiling allowed a wealth of light through the windows. She had bought the condo for the east-facing exposure. Bright sunlight flooded her place in the mornings. The perfect time to paint. Doused in that light now, she examined every inch of the back side.

Nothing.

Question after question cascaded in her mind. Along with an inescapable dread. The painting, *her father's painting*, was connected to the dead man in the chair. There was no denying that now. And the note?

The wall clock chimed. She'd been at the condo longer than expected. Absently, she glanced at the door. Reporters could be lurking. She wrestled with taking the painting to her mother's. The last thing she needed was more evidence at her condo connecting her to Sam Wood. No one could know about what she'd discovered on the back of the painting. Her stomach lurched.

After rifling through her closet, she tossed clothes into a duffel bag. Taking the elevator down to the parking garage, she picked up her mail and tossed the handful onto the passenger seat. She backed out and looped down to the first level. As she hit daylight, she noticed one letter had slipped off the seat onto the floorboard.

Square envelope. Handwritten. No return address.

Nina pulled to the curb and shifted into park. She snatched the envelope. Inside was a piece of torn newsprint. No byline.

*Gallery Owner Bristles. Collaboration Exhibit Sketchy at Best*

———————— •━━ ————————

Nina walked into Tisha's house holding the clipping in one hand, the duffel bag in the other. She'd left *Paris Bench* stowed safely in the trunk.

"What's that face for?" Tisha, sitting on the couch, glanced up from the crystals gathered in her lap. She shifted her glasses, nesting in her hair, onto her nose.

"A news article." Nina stepped closer, turned the paper so Tisha could read the print.

"I don't get it."

Nina flipped it over, reread the headline. "Why would someone send this to me?"

"Could it be about the man in the chair? I think you should call the police."

"And ask for more interrogation?" She stuffed the clipping back inside the envelope. "No, thanks." She spun away.

"It could be evidence. Something the police should look into."

Nina wasn't biting. She had the painting to contend with and the note. That was enough. Considering the newspaper clipping too? All of it circumstantial. But like crumbs, gather enough of them and a clump forms. A clump that couldn't be ignored.

"Withholding evidence." Tisha warned and tossed in a "Tsk, tsk."

Nina, near exasperation, turned back about to respond, but Tisha was in her zone, as she liked to call it. In her palm sat a white, translucent stone with striations. Eyes closed, she began chanting.

"What are you doing, Mother?"

Tisha opened one eye. "Selenite will quiet our minds. Wipe away negative energy."

"While you're doing that, I'll call the Psychic Friends Network." Nina shook her head and huffed to her room.

Sitting on the bed, she scooted against the headboard and let out a sigh. Fishing her cell phone from the duffel, she called Jack.

"You got a minute?" she asked after he picked up.

"Just a few between patients."

"Something came in the mail today. Odd, really. Just a folded newspaper clipping." She read it to him.

"Did you call the police?" Jack asked.

"Not you too." She punched the pillow on her lap.

"Call the police, Nina. People don't just send anonymous newspaper clippings. There's a reason. I'm no lawyer, but withholding evidence is a crime."

"How do we even know it's evidence?" She knew she was being unreasonable. The last thing she wanted was to fan the fires connecting her to Sam Wood. She wanted it all to go away. She wanted to paint again and punch a time card at the gallery. None of that was possible until she cleared her name. After a weighty pause, she agreed through gritted teeth. She would call the police.

Thoughts of talking to Kanoy brought heartburn. He had a knack for getting under her skin, pinning her down like a common criminal, making her feel defensive and small. And that smirk. Nina felt her pulse quickening as she punched in the precinct's number. She attempted to rally confidence by sitting taller, leaning into the headboard, and stretching her feet out. She wasn't his punching bag, yet she felt that way as soon as he answered.

"Detective Kanoy, Nina Shubert. I'm calling about the Sam Wood incident." *There. Concise. Commanding. I'm in the driver's seat.*

"Glad you called." He cleared his throat. "Ms. Shubert, nice to hear from you."

Yep, he was wearing that smirk.

"You came up in a meeting this morning. New developments. We need you to come in ASAP."

Nina slumped against the headboard and closed her eyes.

# TWENTY-TWO

Tisha insisted on driving. Though it wasn't a particularly cloudy day, Nina wore sunglasses to hide her irritation.

The precinct sat a block from The Galleries. On the back side, though, the same street as the hotel. Passing the Caspian brought bitterness and regret. The two were entwined in a nightmare. There was nothing black and white about what had happened. She'd never lived in the gray of life and felt off-kilter. She popped a mint. She'd sucked down a wine cooler, the only alcohol Nina could find in Tisha's fridge.

"Can you sense the spirits here?" Tisha glanced out the windshield like they were on a sightseeing trip. "Always wanted to stay at the Caspian," she said as they passed.

Nina pulled down her glasses, and her eyes drilled into Tisha. "Really?" Her tongue felt thick, her stomach sour, despite the sweet mint. "Let's talk about what I'm telling Kanoy." Nina angled in the seat toward Tisha.

"The Pie-pie shop owner—what's her name?"

"Piper."

"She says the food is wonderful at the Caspian. Did you try the ribs? Piper treated her employees to lunch there last Christmas—"

"Mother. Let's stay on topic." Nina slid back into the middle of the seat, exhausted, and they hadn't even arrived at the police station. She glanced out the window and rolled her eyes. They'd just pulled into the parking lot.

"Let's hurry inside. I've never cared for this block." Tisha turned off the car. "Creepy vibes." She scooted out of the car.

Nina must have driven by the police station a thousand times without a second thought. The unremarkable square, brick building looked like a corporate headquarters or a Kinko's with stylish executive suites upstairs. Knowing it was the precinct where Kanoy plotted against her made the building appear dark and menacing.

A petite woman with a flowery dress ushered them up a flight of stairs that reeked of pot. Nina refused to hold the handrail and grabbed Tisha's hand when she considered doing just that.

Upstairs, a handful of messy desks cramped the room. "Here," the woman offered without intonation and drifted away.

They settled into the plastic chairs. Between the phones buzzing at various octaves and doors slamming, Nina couldn't gather her own thoughts, much less decide what she would divulge to Kanoy. It wasn't just the newspaper clipping or *Paris Bench* with Sam Wood's name on it that she considered sharing. It wouldn't take much for Kanoy to figure out the connection with her father. All of it more than coincidence.

She was wringing her hands. She looked at Tisha, who was digging in her purse. She wished Jack was there. He would tell her everything would be fine. Whether that was true or not, she desperately needed to hear it.

Voices carried, including that of a belligerent teen in handcuffs several desks down. The room smelled of sweat and mischief. Nina focused on the desk in front of them. Tucked between a stack of binders and a stained Broncos mug she spotted a nameplate. *Carol Kanoy.* She couldn't help smiling. Carol. No doubt the source of his prickly disposition.

Another smell caught her attention. A perfume, maybe. Expensive and floral. Nina glanced right, and there she was: Odilia, trailing behind Kanoy. They stopped at the door leading to the stairway. Odilia, wearing a tailored long coat over trousers, appeared overdressed and cheerful. She swung her head back laughing at some remark Kanoy made. While he was plucking something—a business card, maybe—from his dress shirt pocket, Odilia slid a glance at Nina. The knowing smile, brief and sharp, quickly returned to Kanoy with rapt attention.

With a sweeping gesture, Kanoy held the door open, and Odilia exited. Kanoy strolled up to Nina, unaware she had witnessed their interaction.

"Ms. Shubert," he boomed. He stuck out a hand and offered a crooked half smile. Nina introduced her mother and waited, her heart tapping a solid beat.

Kanoy settled into his chair and opened a drawer. Noisily, he shuffled around before pulling out an envelope of his own. This one manila and clearly marked *Evidence.*

He tilted the envelope. An object dropped into his palm, and he jiggled it like a die before holding it between his fingers.

"A crystal," Tisha announced brightly. "Chalcedony, I believe."

"Huh." Kanoy examined the stone. "I'll be damned. Looks like a plain old rock." He turned his attention back to the ladies. "We found it in Sam Wood's front pocket." Kanoy dropped the stone back into the envelope. "We questioned Odilia about the finding." His eyes held a slight glimmer. "The wife generally knows what her husband buries in his pockets." He scratched behind his ear. "Odilia." He repeated her name like a foreign phrase he'd just learned and liked the way it rolled off his thin lips.

Nina, attentive as Kanoy spoke, couldn't help noticing his mouth when he said her name. Odilia. Forming a perfect O with those lizard lips. The same as Sam Wood's when she had found him. Had he cried out for his wife? Like a dying man on the battlefield begs for his mother? Had Sam loved his wife with such devotion that in his final seconds all he could mutter was her name?

With deliberately slow movements, Kanoy rested his elbows on the desk, laced his fingers, and leaned forward. "Back to you ladies." A sugary smile followed. "Why would Sam Wood have a crystal in his pocket? Odilia thought I should ask you." He shifted to Tisha, a slight accusatory squint pulling his eyes. "How did you know it was a crystal?"

# TWENTY-THREE

"I'll admit . . ." Jack fumbled with his chopsticks. "When you texted me *I did it*, I thought you were talking about killing Sam Wood." He finally snagged an egg roll from the flimsy carton and held it up proudly.

"Really?" Nina, stuck on the accusatory comment, ignored the egg roll and glanced at Jack like he was crazy. They were at The Fishing Hole, juggling cashew chicken, chow mein, and egg roll cartons on their laps.

"So Tisha admitted she sold crystals?" Jack, hiding a smile, shook his head.

Nina was swirling noodles in the sweet and sour sauce. "She opened her purse and brought out a healing kit and dumped the pouch on Kanoy's desk."

Jack laughed. "What did he do?"

"Tisha was pointing to rose quartz and saying how it could help in the romance department when he abruptly stood and slammed the drawer on his finger."

"Ouch." Jack grimaced. He gave up on the chopsticks and reached for a fork. He paused, looked at Nina. "I haven't laughed like this in a while." A quick touch of his full belly, and he reconsidered the fork. In the end, he rested the fork on a napkin. He sighed, slumped back in the chair, and sipped from a water bottle. "You're not like my usual patients."

She began closing cartons, aware of his gaze watching her every movement and doing her best to ignore him.

"Wish I could snap my fingers and figure out who killed Sam Wood."

Nina glanced up. Jack's face was drawn and serious. Too serious. She was enjoying the brief escape from real life.

Finally, Jack managed a tiny smile. "I'm glad you picked me to solve the puzzle." He crossed his leg, backtracked. "Not exactly a puzzle, I know." His gaze drifted to the fish tank as if he didn't want her to see something in his eyes. "Doing this with you has kept me distracted from other things."

He didn't elaborate, which was fine. The gurgle of the fish tank had become music of sorts. She was happy to sit, holed up here, away from the reality of Kanoy's men in the shadows. One of them, she was sure, would eventually nab her. Somehow, that no longer felt distant, like a what-if. More of a when.

As if sensing her lost in thought, Jack cleared his throat, startling her.

"You have a patient?"

He shook his head. "I was wondering what's next."

Of course. The case superseded anything else. For a fraction of a moment, she thought he meant them. What was next with them. Why had that possibility entered her thoughts? She dismissed the silliness and reached for her purse. From the side pocket, she withdrew the newspaper clipping and stared at it for a time, unsure if she should show him.

"What do you think?" she finally asked and handed it over.

He read the headline. "Did you tell Kanoy?"

"We never got to it." She grabbed her index finger, reenacting the painful drawer slam. "He had told us the preliminary autopsy was complete and they were waiting on the report. Then he slammed his finger." *Autopsy*. The word twisted in her mouth.

Jack read the headline again. "It could be harmless." He shrugged. "But how can we dismiss it? Gallery. Exhibit." He pressed his lips together. "Someone's trying to get your attention. No doubt about Sam Wood." He sought out her eyes, which she immediately diverted. It irked her that Jack had agreed with Tisha. Agreeing with her mother broke some unwritten code. Then, like a girl who followed rules, she let Jack's words percolate.

He turned over the envelope and examined the postmark. "We could poke around," he said hopefully, raising an unruly eyebrow. "Broadmoor? The outskirts of the Springs. Isn't that thirty, forty minutes from here?"

"At least." It wasn't that far. Nina snatched back the envelope. "I'm going, Jack."

He looked at her with surprise. "Not without me."

"You have patients," she reminded him.

A rush of air left his lungs. "Remember, I'm down to three days. Since Cam . . ." His voice trailed off.

"Cam?" she whispered.

"Yeah. My five-year-old boy. Not an ounce of Frank in him. Spitting image of his mom." A closed-lip smile followed. Forced, maybe. No, a cover-up for despair. "Gwen left when Cam was two." Jack swigged water, wiped his mouth with the back of his hand. "A creek runs through my backyard. A trickle most summers. Winter's another story. Somehow Cam slipped out the back door. Must have fallen or stumbled on a boulder. The police weren't definite about the actual cause." He slugged back the last of the water. "Doesn't matter, really." He tossed the empty in the trash can. "He's gone."

Nina reached over, squeezed his shoulder.

"Honestly, Nina, I'm just making time here." His glance shifted to the rickety cabinets. On the countertops below sat dingy file boxes with broken lids. Black marker scratched out words and dates. Other words were written below. *Patient Folders. Taxes. Child Frames.* "I check people's eyes. Fit them with glasses or contacts."

"You're more than that." She smiled, though he wasn't looking at her. His eyes drifted over Nina's shoulder, to the fish tank.

Nina swung a quick glance over her shoulder. A lone picture hung crookedly on the wall. A tow-haired boy stood in a field of wild grass, poking his head through the tall reeds, making googly eyes.

Jack choked down a gasp, wiped a hand below his nose. "The thing is . . ." Legs spread, he ducked his head down, choking back tears. "I mean, the truth is, I'm not sure I locked the back door before going to bed the night Cam drowned in the creek."

# TWENTY-FOUR

Nina could have easily driven to Broadmoor alone. And a part of her wanted to. To prove the headline meant nothing. Her reasoning, she realized, wouldn't bring her closer to finding the killer. The headline *was* a lead. In her gut, she knew that. Admitting it to herself was entirely different.

As a child, she had lived in Broadmoor. She hadn't told Jack and didn't plan to. What was the point? She remembered nothing about the town. Only her tiny sphere: the house she had lived in and a few shops in town.

By nine the next morning, she and Jack were on the road. Returning to Broadmoor felt daunting. A weight of sorts left her groggy and pinned to the car seat.

The more she tried to distract herself, the more her thoughts swirled around Sam Wood's name on the back of *Paris Bench*. She still couldn't believe Sam claimed to be the owner of the painting. That hit deep. Like a catapult sinking the very object she'd built her career on. Was it conceivable that he had picked *her* out of thousands who had applied with The Artist Network? Wasn't the process anonymous? Like other contests, she had been assigned a number. Could he have somehow rigged the judging?

As the city whirred by, with it, her confidence slipped out the window. She gulped down water and tried focusing on the blur of land. The low hills, potato brown. The tawny brush stark against the open sky. All of it drawing her deeper into an edgy fright. A place she'd never been.

To distract herself, she googled directions. Two galleries popped up. Nina blew out a breath. They were almost there. "Looks like Pine Gallery is on the way into town," she told Jack. "Stop there first?" He nodded.

She couldn't find the beauty in the land, now jagged slopes, rugged grasslands. All of it harsh and isolated. A cavern of what-ifs hid in the rise, just over the hill. What if her name wasn't cleared? What if she never painted again? What if her father found out? She imagined telling him. He would have tried his best to hold a smile, but his eyes would betray him. She looked at Jack, wishing she could share about her father and what had happened. He glanced over and she attempted a smile. Concern clouded his eyes. Maybe she'd been too quiet, or he sensed her body tensing. It seemed the closer they got to Broadmoor, the more nervous she became.

"Have you thought about what you're going to say at the gallery?" Jack asked.

"I'm not sure." She hadn't thought that far.

"You always have brilliant ideas." Jack shot her a playful look, trying to coax her out of her funk. It worked, at least in that moment. "Says the doctor with a degree on the wall." He grinned and pulled to the curb. "If the galleries don't pan out, let's try the local newspaper. They should have the article."

And that was what they did. Neither gallery had any recollection of the article. Nina had tossed out her father's name and even Sam

Wood's. Between owner changes and twentysomethings minding the stores, they struck out.

They ducked into a bagel joint to figure out their next step. Jack slid her half of his bagel across the table. Nina shook her head. She couldn't eat and opted for a cuppa. While Nina nursed the breakfast tea, Jack questioned the sassy kid behind the counter. *Butte County Newspaper* in Broadmoor distributed its newspaper countywide. Between the caffeine and the expectation of reading the article, Nina's heart was thudding in her chest. Or the caffeine on an empty stomach had run its course. "Let's go." Nina snuck the last bagel bite and practically pulled Jack off the chair.

A few streets over, tall, wooden storefronts lined the main drag. Some with a Wild West vibe. Or *Westworld.* The rise of blue pines climbed up the mountain in the distance.

*The Butte County News* sat between a taffy shop and Paul's Print Shop. *TBCN* was written in a large font below Paul's sign. Paul, a tall, willowy man with faded jeans and a slight limp, served double duty and directed them to a shoebox-size archive room at the back. He stood in front of a wall-to-ceiling cabinet of tiny drawers. "What date are you looking for?"

Jack and Nina looked at each other, dumbfounded. In all their excitement, they hadn't thought about *when* the article had been written. She retrieved the newspaper clipping from her purse and examined it. No date. She handed it to Paul.

"Hmm." He scratched behind his ear. "Collaboration?" A slow grin followed. "Nice play on words, don't you think?"

"Any ideas?" Jack asked impatiently. They just wanted answers.

Paul, still smiling, seemed to be savoring the moment. "I don't know the specifics," he admitted and then stabbed the clipping with his finger. "This happened here at Crescent Moon Gallery."

"We didn't see Crescent Moon Gallery on Google," Nina said.

"Recently changed names." Paul's giddiness, apparently for being in the know, lingered.

Jack snatched the clipping. "Thank you." He grazed the square of Nina's back, ushering her outside.

They hurried back to the main strip of shops and perched on a bench to get their bearings. The afternoon sun beamed down on them. Learning the name of the gallery felt like a win. Yet every step forward meant they were closer to the truth. Was she ready for that? She grabbed her phone and held it in a shady spot between them and punched in Crescent Moon Gallery.

"The internet's slow." She glanced up, sheltering her eyes. "We've got to be close." Her eyes darted up and down the street: Touristy stores. A museum, a real estate office. A fudge shop. Then she saw it, just over Jack's shoulder. "We're really close." Anticipation caught in her throat. And something else, a sour taste. Not quite like the smells that came along with the odd sensations, but enough to make her wary.

# TWENTY-FIVE

Remnants of a lazy sunset shimmered behind the Crescent Moon Gallery. To prepare for a special evening showing, the gallery had closed until dusk. Biding time, Nina and Jack shared a ham and cheese sammie and a bag of chips at a deli. Nina picked at her half.

"You're not eating." He stuffed down the last of his half before jiggling the open bag of chips. A handful scattered onto the napkin. He lifted a chip to her lips. One eyebrow rose playfully.

She pulled away from the table. "I can't look at food." Nervous energy somersaulted in her belly. "Yours." She slid her half across the table and checked her cell phone for the time. It seemed to be passing in slow motion.

"If you're not eating, I'm done too." Jack wrapped the remains in a napkin and tossed the lot in the trash can. "Come on." He motioned with a hand. "Let's mosey over. Maybe they'll open a few minutes early."

Outside the gallery's glass doors, they peered in like school-children anxious for the bell to ring. Once inside, Nina breathed in polished wood and the tang of varnish. Familiar smells. The gallery felt like an old friend. She licked her lips, wanting to explore, gaze at the paintings, acquaint herself with the artists, subject matter, and style of each artwork as if she'd slipped into her role at The Art Loft. But this wasn't her gallery, and the momentary fascination faded.

She needed a drink.

They passed the trio of musicians pinched in a corner in front of the picture window and headed toward the bar perched at the back of the gallery and ordered. With a whiskey in hand, she tapped Jack's Stella. "To finding answers." *I hope.* Nina briefly smiled. She lifted the tumbler and sipped.

"I'm optimistic." Jack tossed back the bottle and glanced around. They were the first ones there. A tad awkward. Usually, she enjoyed music at a showing. The addition, light and often peppy tunes, raised the fun level. Drinks and jazz, Stacey often said, sold paintings.

Tonight, the slim fellow plucking the cello sounded monotonous; the violin, pitchy. Nina quickly strolled by them. She'd spotted the gallery owner. She knew the look. Formally dressed and fussing with a frame on what looked to be the feature wall soaring into the rafters. A spotlight illuminated tonight's star: a ginormous multimedium piece in primary colors.

He turned, his eyes bright and expectant. Customers, he thought, Nina was sure. She hated to burst his bubble. She smiled widely, sauntered up to the man in the too-tight suit. "Lovely gallery you have." Her eyes traveled the painting, an appearance of awe widening her gaze. "A new piece?" she asked. "The colors are vibrant."

Like a proud papa, his chest opened, and he rocked back on his heels. Nina allowed him a minute to soak up the sugary accolades before diving in. "I heard a local paper carried a story about your gallery years back." She decided against whipping out the headline. "A showing, just like this." She glanced around, looking pleased at the setup. As she suspected, he noticed her sweeping gaze and bright eyes. "A collaboration of some sort that went south?"

"You're talking mid-eighties?" The man padded over to a bank of light switches and fiddled with knobs. "Not a brawl." He surveyed the lights above, adjusted their strength. "Two fellas were disrupting my patrons. Pissed me off." He pressed a hand against his paisley tie and sucked in his belly.

"Do you remember their names?" Jack asked.

"Can't seem to recall." Another couple entered. "Excuse me," he said politely.

Before he could step away, Nina blurted out, "Could one of them have been Sam Wood or Cyrus Shubert?" She held her breath.

"That was a long time ago." He shrugged. "Sorry."

"One more question."

Irritation tugged at Big Belly's lips.

"What was the issue that night?" She needed something.

A cluster of ladies strolled in, drawing his attention. Clasping his lapels, he adjusted his ill-fitting suit jacket. "Listen, I've got customers." He sighed. "All I can tell you is two men were arguing about a painting. The older one hijacked the painting mid-showing and stormed out." He strutted off and then suddenly stopped and turned around. "You people keep coming by asking about that fellow." He frowned. "Please tell me this is the last time." His cheeks prickled red. No doubt the bright lights and the monkey suit.

Nina, confused, stepped closer. "Who asked? She didn't know which fellow he was referring to—Sam, her father, or someone else. "And when?"

"I don't know when." He shrugged. "A year ago, maybe. Same questions. This guy wanted details. Full names, where they lived, that sort of thing."

"Do you remember his name?"

He glanced at the door, watching the women now ogle over a sculpture. That seemed to pacify him and grant Nina a few more moments. "I can barely remember my kids' names." If that was supposed to be funny, it fell flat. Nina's eyes pinned him under the maze of track lighting. He wiped at a bead of sweat below his nose. "You two aren't going to give up." His gaze bounced around the gallery. Something surfaced and he took a deep breath. "The guy wore a pizza logo on his shirt. I've seen him around. Think he lives in the area. That's the best I can do."

Nina wanted to hug him. Not really, but the intention was heartfelt. "Appreciate your time." She drained her glass. Another lead.

Jack caught the gleam in her eye and reached for her hand. On the way out, they deposited their empties at the bar. Jack tucked a five-spot into the tip jar and nodded a thank-you to the bartender, who said, "Heard you talking to Stan about the squabble back in the eighties."

Nina's eyes lit up.

The bartender poured a shot of dark rum into a tumbler. "My aunt worked here back then. She mentioned the altercation a time or two." He slid an orange slice around the rim before dropping it in the drink.

Jack and Nina exchanged glances. "Where can we find her?"

# TWENTY-SIX

Skylar Whippler worked at Mighty Dream Books. According to the bartender, the craftsman house turned kids' bookstore was an iconic fixture in Broadmoor dating back to the fifties.

Jack and Nina stood outside the gallery. "You up for this?" he asked.

A streetlamp flashed on above them. Store windows now dark, the town appeared empty. One car was parked on the street. Theirs. Jack glanced at his watch. "Too late to scour the pizza joints here in Butte. And no bookstore would be open this late."

Her mind skipped right over the bookstore. "How are we going to find the pizza guy?" It seemed daunting. "Are we going to question every man with a pizza logo on his shirt?" They didn't have much to go on. That reality was setting in, or maybe she was just tired.

Jack looked up the street into the blackness, toward the highway. "Seems crazy to drive down the mountain tonight, return here tomorrow."

Home wasn't that far away. It seemed that way, though. Traversing rugged terrain at night didn't sound appealing. The day had caught up to her. But spending the night here? With Jack?

Jack must have read her expression. "Two rooms, of course." When she didn't respond, he fought to hide a smile. "Separate floors?"

Nina spun toward the road leading out of town. Inky black. Desolate. Turning back to Jack, his craggy smile lightened any perceived awkwardness. He had a way of chipping away at her serious side. Always professional regardless of the circumstances, she honestly didn't know how to shed that part of her. It was hardwired into her DNA. She didn't know how to be any other way.

When Nina nodded, Jack grinned wide and scooted along the sidewalk searching for a hotel.

The Old Towne Inn, a brick two-story with black shutters and a wheelbarrow of yellow chrysanthemums, had rooms. While Jack secured them, Nina perched on a chair inside the empty foyer. Sidelong glances followed Jack to the front desk. Nina shifted in the chair, feeling uneasy being here with him. Was it that or staying in Broadmoor? Something skittered in her chest. She flicked at a button on her blouse, adjusting the fabric. Her heartbeat felt off or heavy, like a piano playing the wrong notes.

Jack strolled up with the keys. She clutched her purse and silently followed. On the stairs, she purposefully lagged. At the top of the stairs, he fumbled with the old-fashioned key, missing the lock altogether. He almost laughed and then gave it another try.

When the door swung open, Nina reached for the key. Fragrant sweet and citrus scents wafted from the room. Their eyes locked. By far the deepest connection they'd shared. Nina could hear his breath mingling in the space between them. A question dangled unanswered. The moment passed. His fingertips let go, and the key slid from his hand to hers.

"Sleep tight." He lifted a hand to wave, then seemed to think better of it and shoved it in his pocket. Walking backward, a tiny smile played on his lips as he tossed his own key back and forth between his hands.

"Good night, Jack." Nina was blushing. Not that she was prudish in any way. She regarded relationships like paintings. You started by taping down the watercolor paper. Then you drew a fairly detailed sketch. Next, you mixed colors, *many* colors, before you began to paint. With Jack, none of that existed. The accusation of murder superseded any chance at normalcy. She kept telling herself that, pushing down any budding feelings for Jack. The feeling in her chest returned, and she glanced down at her clothing.

"Meet you in the lobby. I'll be the one wearing a blue blouse, sweater, and blue jeans."

---

Nina awoke bounding with energy and a dry mouth. She desperately needed tea and to beat Jack to the lobby. She didn't feel human before a strong English Breakfast kicked in. She was nursing a cup when Jack coursed down the stairs.

"Glad I spotted the white sweater," he tossed out, making his way to the coffee and pouring a to-go cup. He glanced around before stuffing two packaged muffins in his pocket. With a nod toward the door, Nina grabbed her tea.

"What did people do before Google?" She found five pizza places within the city limits. They nixed restaurants that served pizza and Italian food. Jack agreed that Italian restaurants wouldn't have a pizza-specific logo.

Way too early for restaurants to open, they settled on a bench and leisurely sipped their steaming beverages. Nina sensed the town awakening as merchants opened doors. Cars began arriving. The tea had settled her nerves, and the sun had claimed the day.

Jack leaned over, eyed the pizza places showing on the phone. "Noni's. I like the sound of that one."

"We should start at the top. Cambiano's."

Jack gulped down the coffee. "Rule-follower," he teased. "What if we find him at Noni's?" He waited, seemingly expecting a witty comeback.

She had none. Nina frowned. "Noni's, then. Let's go." They started walking. "Let's check out the restaurant signage first."

"Agreed. No pizza slice, no go." Jack reached for her hand and picked up the pace.

"If we go in acting like Kanoy, the workers will clam up. Maybe we should make small talk first." Nina slowed, looked at Jack. "You're good at that." He was much better than her at making people feel comfortable. She had to work at it daily. "And let's pick someone who's worked there a few years."

Jack stopped, cupped her cheeks tenderly, and slipped in close. "We'll figure this out." He smiled. "Any more talk of how this is going to play out and I'm turning back." He winked.

Three pizza joints later, no luck. No pizza slice logo or facsimile. When possible, they had spoken to the owner and dropped Sam's and Cyrus's names, along with the gallery incident. Anything to jog their minds.

Feeling defeated and hungry, Jack plucked a muffin from his pocket. Nina rolled her eyes. "Really?" Hardly satisfying after smelling pizza joints prepping for the lunch rush. "Pizza seems the obvious choice."

"Smart woman."

Nina checked her list for the next closest joint. She glanced up at the street signs to get her bearings. "This way." She pointed.

As she stepped off the curb to cross the street, a raucous crowd rounded the corner and engulfed them. A parade of some sort. Nina stumbled back against Jack, who wrapped both arms around her to steady them against the cloud of bodies. Unable to move, he steered their upper bodies away from a tipsy woman holding a wineglass at a precarious tilt. Jack, doing his best, hopscotched through the mob with Nina in tow. Finally, he ushered them out of the throng, onto the street. Now paralleling the crowd, the GPS signaled their destination. Of course, it was on the other side of the crowd. Nina stood on her toes. She couldn't see any sign on the buildings above the horde.

Nina reached for Jack's hand. They dodged bodies before creeping out onto the sidewalk in front of a bare-bones walk-up pizza order window.

"Huh." Nina shrugged. Not exactly what she had expected. Jack snatched a menu off the counter. Hunger, frustration, whatever you call it, they were both on edge.

Nina barely glanced at the menu. "Margherita or barbecue chicken sounds good."

Jack frowned. A straggler from the crowd brushed against them, and Jack eased them closer to the order window. "Barbecue chicken isn't pizza," he argued. He slipped a hand over her back just as a high-heeled gal nearly drifted into Nina. "Pepperoni. That's a pizza!" He was shouting above the hoopla. Nina jerked the flimsy menu from his hand just as a kid latched on to Jack's leg, stumbling forward and falling in front of them.

"Whoa." Jack pulled the boy up by the straps crossing his back. Fully garbed in a helmet and skates, the chunk of a hockey player lifted his chin up at Jack. The black helmet covered his eyes, leaving a button nose and ruddy cheeks.

"Excuse me," a small voice uttered. He tugged at his jersey tucked down inside padded black pants. Now smooth and hanging straight, the shirt's logo became clear. The Crested Coyotes. Inside the circle, a ravenous coyote devoured a slice of pizza.

Jack squatted. "Okay, bud?" He adjusted the helmet to expose the kid's eyes, curious and the deepest shade of green. Jack looked him over, smiled. "Hockey, huh. A tough-guy sport."

He looked to be about seven or eight. *Close to Cam's age,* Nina thought.

The boy didn't say much. He seemed more interested in chewing on his mouth guard between nods. Jack stood, glanced over his shoulder. "Pizza any good here?"

"Gramps makes the best." His words came out garbled behind the thick face shield.

Looking at Nina above the boy's sight line, Jack's eyebrows rose. He touched the boy's padded shoulder. "Can we meet Gramps?"

They followed the tyke along a back alley between buildings to a door leading down to a basement. Inside, a glow of light lit a sliver of a brick room. Jack navigated down three steps, bent to see below the slanted roof before waving Nina to follow.

"Your grandson said I might find the owner of The Pizza Store down here," Jack called out into the dank space. He glanced over his shoulder for the boy. He had disappeared.

The sound of dripping water echoed up the stairs, followed by a grunt.

"Hello?" Jack glanced back at Nina and shrugged.

Another grunt. "You better be Joey's buddy with the snake."

Jack shuffled farther down the steps. "Sorry." Seeing the man hunkered over a drainpipe, he winced. "Will an extra pair of hands help? I'm Jack," he said, reaching out a hand.

The nearly bald man had wisps of black hair; wide, lifeless eyes; and a gravelly voice. "Luca." He straightened up, wrestled with a wrench. He didn't appear keen on talking to them and shifted the tap, tightened this and that.

"We . . ." Jack motioned a hand up the stairs where Nina had remained. "We were at the Crescent Moon Gallery last night." He crept down to the uneven brick landing. "The owner said you were asking questions about Sam Wood."

Nina carefully navigated the stairs and joined Jack. "You knew Sam?" she asked.

Luca wiped his hands with a dingy cloth. "I knew he was up to something. The bastard stole from me." He glanced skyward. "Some restaurant I have. The twerp screwed me. This was supposed to rival my brother's place up the street, Cassini's." He tossed the rag on the counter. A white flag of sorts. "A window to sell pizza. Pfft."

Nina was having a tough time finding sympathy. She knew, though, that a kind word could bring answers. If he had murdered Sam, she needed to tread lightly. No sane person would come right out and say it. "Tough break," she started. "Sorry to hear what happened to you. I can't imagine how you felt after he stole your dreams." Was she making things worse, fueling his anger? She let the words settle in the damp, cramped space.

Luca dropped a hand under the sink and fiddled, the groan of pipes leaking into the cellar. "It wasn't money," he grunted.

*A painting? No.* Luca didn't seem like a man interested in art. "Then what?" she asked.

"Listen, you're on my dime. Spit out your questions, and let me get to fixin' this money pit."

Momentarily flustered, Nina looked at Jack, who prompted her to continue. She swallowed, struggled to find her train of thought. "The gallery owner said you had asked about Sam?"

"Sam? Huh. I conveniently forgot his name." Luca ducked under the sink. "Maybe we had a conversation one night and he stole a grand right before my eyes." He slid on his side, monkeyed with something. "Well, not exactly right before my eyes. The point is, he screwed me over."

Jack got to the point. "Enough to want to kill him?"

Luca shimmied out from under the sink. "Let's just say I got him back."

"You care to elaborate?" Jack pressed.

Luca slowly rose like an old man with aches and a back that no longer straightened. "And put this gold mine in jeopardy?" He laughed. "Over a schmuck? Hell no."

"Anything you could tell us would help. The police think I murdered Sam." A foul smell leached from the drain. Nina fought a gag reflex and shivered. She was desperate. He had admitted to doing something. But what? She wondered how far she could press him. "There must be something you can tell us." She sidled up to Jack. Without realizing it, their fingers entwined.

Luca fished a handful of muck out of the drain and held it up. "Sam's dead, you say?" With his back to them, he leaned deep into the sink bowl and began humming.

Talking with Luca had only brought unanswered questions. They were guessing what could have happened. Nothing concrete to go on left them frustrated and all talked out.

The bookstore became their focus. She could almost see it in her mind, a grand stately place, yet she never knew it existed. The vision kept popping up. Nina kept dismissing it and redirecting her thoughts to the reason for their visit. Skylar. The fizz of excitement to get there soon faded, replaced by something dark and visceral. Something she couldn't explain.

A jumble of curves on a one-lane road led them to the sprawl of town near jagged slopes edging a reserve. Jack turned the corner, and the bookstore came into view. Nina immediately felt nauseous. She dismissed it, leaned another way in the seat, and stretched her legs.

The pristine craftsman perched on a mound of luscious lawn. Quaint and cozy, the bookstore, with forest-green trim against stark-white siding, bordered on postcard perfect. At least that's what the artist in her thought. Yet every time she eyed the house, her stomach rolled.

Once parked, Jack turned to her. "What's wrong?" Wrinkles mapped his forehead.

"Maybe something I ate. The pizza?" She was holding her stomach, wishing they hadn't wolfed down a slice after leaving Luca. "It will pass," she assured him and slid out of the car, aware of every which way her body shifted.

They began walking toward the bookstore. But it didn't pass. She was rubbing a hand over her belly when an odd sense of déjà vu, mixed with a palpable fright, came at her from all sides. Thready breaths caught in her throat. A slow burn flushed her cheeks. She couldn't choke out any words. She was focusing on her queasiness.

Head slumped, she followed the sidewalk. One step in front of the other. It was the best she could do.

Jack had stopped. They were standing at the steps leading up to the door. Six steps, exactly. Jack started up, but she couldn't lift a leg, much less heft her frame upward. A peculiar feeling pulsed through her, cementing her in place.

With effort, she lifted her head higher toward the gable arching above the door. Its shadow seemed to engulf her. She felt small and alone and lost before everything went dark.

---

Light dappled the wall. The pattern reminded her of a string of pearls. Like the painting *A Young Woman Standing at a Virginal.* Vermeer had painted the pearls translucent, blending into the woman's skin. Nina blinked. The pearls disappeared. Rather, morphed into something else. She rubbed her eyes and blinked again.

She was in a room, she realized, with a chandelier of opulent crystals casting light onto a wall of . . . books? *The bookstore.* With a start, she sat up. "Jack?"

He appeared out of nowhere. Maybe he'd been there all along. "Tea?" He handed her a dainty cup, his fingers too large to grasp the delicate curve of the handle.

Knees to her chest, she took the cup and cradled the warmth. "How long have I been sleeping?" Everything appeared fuzzy. She couldn't quite clear the cobwebs.

"You were out, Nina." He tucked in beside her on the formal chaise lounge. "You passed out." Concern hardened his stare as if he might find a reason for what happened by simply looking at her. "I considered taking you to the hospital."

She took a long sip. And another. The fog began to lift. She remembered the road trip. The newspaper. The gallery. The bartender with kind eyes. Her senses heightened when she recalled what the bartender had said: his aunt had worked at the gallery in the eighties. Nina couldn't remember her name. Then again, she was bad at names.

They were sitting beside a sash window. Outside, a bright sky begged for a playful walk. Inside, shadows hid between the bookcases, appearing cavernous, fading into an abyss. The bookstore was eerily quiet. Something felt off.

"Do you remember why we're here?" Jack asked quietly.

"Of course." She sounded irritated that he had asked, like she had forgotten her memory. Which she hadn't.

Jack stiffened at her abrupt answer. When he pulled away, she touched his arm. "Sorry. I'm a grouch when I wake up." She smiled. "Thank you for taking care of me."

Her glance flitted across the room. She rubbed her temple and wondered if she was imagining things. The pattern on the chaise lounge she sat on—fancy, herringbone—seemed familiar. Her hand lazily played with the braid of fabric edging the cushion.

For a time, they sat in silence: Nina sipping her tea; Jack sliding worried glances her way. The caffeine started kicking in, awakening all sorts of nerve endings. And questions flooded in. She turned to Jack. "How did I get in here?" Here being where they sat. The last thing she remembered was walking up to the building.

"My new buddy, Buck. Considering he's the only male on staff, you picked the right day to pass out. He helped me carry you in."

It dawned on Nina no one was *in* the bookstore. "Where is everybody?"

"The bookstore's closed today. Repairs of some sort. Buck came to unlock a few doors for the workers." Jack checked his phone. "When you're feeling okay, we should head home."

"What about the woman?" Of course, she couldn't remember her name. Was it Carla? "Skylar," Nina whispered and stiffened on the chaise lounge. She looked at Jack. "What is Skylar's last name? Does it start with a *W*?"

Jack, reaching for her empty cup, hesitated. "Whip something. Whipple, I think." His eyes grew wide.

"SW," Nina whispered. "Could it be her? Could she have written the note?"

Jack fidgeted with the cup on the saucer, almost upending it. Carefully settling the cup, his fingers froze on the rim as if willing it to stay before letting go. Pleased with himself, no doubt, he looked up with a smile. "Highly doubt Skylar wrote the note."

"Why?"

"I don't know why," was his answer. "Buck said she's on vacation for a few days." He shot Nina a concerned look. "Let's give it a rest. You just woke up from who knows what happened to you. Next week, we'll give her a call." He patted Nina's knee. "Only," he emphasized, "if you're up to it."

Nina racked her brain for any mention of Skylar growing up. No recollection. Only an upset stomach that wouldn't subside. She rubbed her belly. She felt like a child who'd ruined an outing. Their efforts had stalled, and it was her fault. She would talk to Skylar soon. First, though, she needed to get out of this place.

Jack moseyed over to the coffee cart against the wall and returned the cup and saucer. "Let's sit outside on the porch. Give you a minute before we leave." She didn't balk and took his hand when he offered.

"I'm fine, really. A bit tired. That's all." She covered a yawn. But she was far from fine. As soon as she stood up, that icky feeling surfaced.

They meandered along a darkened hallway. The front entrance seemed far away. Fighting vertigo, she was doing her best to focus on the paneled door ahead that would usher her outside. Maybe she had some sort of flu or food poisoning. She needed fresh air, a reclining car seat, and a deep sleep.

The room seemed to stretch out, like in one of those movies where the door grew farther and farther away. They passed a window. Light streamed in and Nina squinted. She followed the wedge of light down onto the polished floor. It wasn't odd, really, but Nina found it confounding and froze.

"What's wrong?" Jack frowned.

The stream of light continued across the hall. A slow, methodical gaze traveled over every groove in the floor because somehow, she knew what she was going to see before she laid eyes on it. Her head snapped up and locked onto a cutout under the stairway. Her heart plummeted. A part of her wanted to sink to the floor and curl into a ball like a roly-poly.

Cheerful pillows and colorful books scattered about the tight space. But standing five feet away, none of it appeared the least bit cheerful. The nook pulled at her, a palpable fear inching up her spine. She couldn't breathe.

Incandescent blues and crimson reds danced in front of her eyes. An explosion of color, harsh and bright. She couldn't quite lock onto what she was seeing. And then, like a kaleidoscope coming into view, she recognized the childlike painting on the wall.

The Eiffel Tower.

# TWENTY-SEVEN

Few knew that at the center of The Galleries, behind Pie-pie, the eye of a labyrinth existed. The Galleries' paths meandered like a circular maze. Most shops were wedged in like pie pieces. Others rose two levels in a Frank Lloyd Wright fashion. A true labyrinth bore a center, often hidden within hedges. After discovering the hidden space behind her restaurant, Piper had placed a bench there. Secluded by overgrown shrubbery, Nina and only a few others knew about the peaceful place.

Three days had passed since visiting Broadmoor. Nina had spent most of that time holed up in Tisha's guest room, ducking out only once to pick up her mail. Now sitting on Piper's bench, hidden from the world, Nina stared at the envelope from The Artist Network. Clouds overhead darkened the crisp envelope, heavy in her hand. Finally, holding her breath, she ripped it open.

The words, succinct and heartless, shattered any hope she had of returning to painting.

*Your membership has been revoked . . . including your recent Best of Show award. Participation of any kind is no longer allowed at the local or state level.*

Nina crumbled the letter. She just sat there, numb, as if the news hadn't affected her. Yet it had. In the bleakness, she appeared unphased. A defense mechanism. The alternative required energy.

Leaves rustled and Nina looked up. One of Piper's workers poked through the shrubs.

"I was just leaving," Nina said, mustering a faint smile. Tucking the wadded letter in her back pocket, she slipped through the narrow gap in the bushes and entered Pie-pie's back door. Intent on avoiding conversation with Piper—or anyone else, for that matter—Nina dragged past the counter, only seeing the feet of patrons' shoes propped on the shiny stool rungs. She knew the restaurant's footprint and could easily make her way to the front door without glancing up.

"Nina Shubert."

She stopped, followed the sound of the familiar grating voice.

Kanoy slouched in a booth, hands bracing a coffee mug. "Lucky me finding you here." Thin lips contorted into a hard smile. "I was about to give you a jingle."

Nina would have stood her ground, but she didn't want everyone hearing Kanoy's blabber. She sauntered over and stood, arms crossed, in front of the booth. She didn't have the energy to look him in the eye.

"Aren't you chipper?"

If he was giving her that smirk, she didn't care. Jaw clenched, she finally looked up. "You have something to tell me?"

"I suggest you hire a lawyer, young lady. We're close." He latched on to the coffee cup and slurped down the liquid, followed by a satisfying "ah." Pushing the cup aside, he leaned in, drilled into her eyes. "Get your things in order."

*Where could she go?*

Nina, shaking, fired up the Prius. This was the time to cry, but she couldn't. Swerving out of The Galleries parking lot, she slammed on the brakes halfway into the street. A biker, inches from her bumper, flipped her off. *Idiot,* he mouthed.

Clutching the steering wheel, she closed her eyes, took a deep breath before motoring on. Only one person came to mind. The one person who accepted her, no matter what.

She pulled up to the modest one-story and parked. She'd never been to Jack's house. He had jotted the address on a napkin one day at The Fishing Hole. *"Come by any time. I mean it. You're always welcome."* Now, looking at the ranch-style house, it wasn't what she had expected. A splintered wood porch in need of a fresh coat of paint. Above, what looked like wood rot across the portico. The house looked plain tired. Like Jack most days. Yet his face lit up when he answered the door, then soured.

"What's wrong?" He ushered her inside, pulled out a chair at a well-worn dining table. She crumbled into it.

"Water? Something stronger?"

In theory, a splash of whiskey sounded perfect. "Water's fine." No amount of alcohol could suppress what had happened today.

Nina attempted a smile. He brought that side out of her. Most perennial optimists shared that knack. Jack slipped in beside her and handed her the glass. She really didn't want the water, but holding it gave her something to do, something to stare at, while Jack listened. The letter. Kanoy. It all flooded out in a wave of despair.

"Why didn't you tell Kanoy about the headline or Stuart?" Jack paused, formed a fist, and rested it on the table. "Give him someone other than you." He jerked away. "I want to help you. Can't you see that?"

She did. And she needed his help more than ever. But she felt betrayed by her own mind. What if something had happened in Sam Wood's hotel room that she didn't remember? As more time passed, the memory of that day had become fragmented. Details were slipping away. She tucked her hair behind her ears. She needed to get a hold of herself, stop the downward spiral.

"Okay." Nina nodded. "I'll call Kanoy."

"No," Jack balked. "After what happened in the bookstore, you need to talk to Skylar first. Maybe we'll have more to tell him."

Not one peep had escaped Jack's mouth on the way home from Broadmoor. She'd slept. Rather, she had forced herself to sleep. Anything to wipe away the image of the Eiffel Tower painting pulsing behind her eyes. No discussion about calling Skylar had surfaced until now.

Nina gulped down the water. She wasn't sure she was ready to uncover any more bad news, assuming Skylar had anything to add to today's pile.

Jack seemed okay with her silence and returned to the kitchen to refill her glass. Nina snuck a peek around the older house. Mishmashed, worn furniture; glass stain rings on the coffee table. And socks poking out from under the couch, resembling a bachelor pad. Except for the wooden time-out bench in the living room.

Jack returned to the table. He'd followed her eyes. "Yeah. Can't seem to get rid of that." He slid the glass toward her. "I keep picturing Cam sitting there, playing with his Transformers." Jack shook his head. "What kid likes the time-out bench?" He let out a long breath, allowing that image to linger before shifting toward her. "What happened at the bookstore?" he asked quietly. "I'd really like to know."

Nina shifted away. "I'm not completely sure." She stood, moseyed to the kitchen sink. She took a long sip and splashed the rest of the water in the sink. "Something familiar gripped me, and it wasn't a good thing." She gazed out the kitchen window. And there it was.

The creek jogging through the backyard. Her hands stilled, and for a moment, she imagined Cam skipping from boulder to boulder.

Her heart hurt.

She returned to the table, unable to look Jack in the eye. She fought a sudden desire to hug him. His trials, she realized, were no less than hers. Her glance drifted to where Jack's cell phone sat on the table.

"Let's call Skylar."

———•—

Nina thumped a finger on the table waiting for Skylar to pick up. Honestly, she dreaded talking to the lady who worked at the bookstore. Rehashing what had happened there, even if just in Nina's mind, was too raw. She didn't dare close her eyes and remember. Nina tried picturing Skylar in a different setting. Anywhere but the bookstore. True, Nina didn't know what Skylar looked like but that's what artists did; use their imagination. Nina tapped the button to put the phone on speaker. She wanted Jack to chime in if she stumbled.

On the third ring, a demure-sounding woman answered. With a flit of her hand, Nina prompted Jack to speak. Jack introduced them and flipped the cell phone in Nina's direction. Before she could utter a word, Skylar blurted out, "You got the headline?"

"It was you?" Nina asked, confused.

"I suspected you'd find me sooner or later." Her voice was breathy, as if she had just returned from a jog.

"Let's start at the beginning," Nina said. "Can you tell us about the article? I'd like to know if it's connected to Sam Wood."

"Bingo," she said in a gasp of breath. "And your father. Don't forget him." Skylar added, surprising Nina. "He's part of this too."

Nina swallowed hard. *What does she know about Dad?* He was off limits. Yet . . . "I want to know everything," she said. For better or worse. Whatever this had to do with her father, she had to know. Nina scooted to the edge of her chair, poised over the phone, waiting.

"Honey, this isn't a phone-call kind of thing."

Nina turned and looked at Jack, who frowned. He was probably thinking the same thing. Returning to Broadmoor wasn't possible. Not after her meltdown. The bookstore, that nook, whatever it was, had spooked her.

"Could we meet halfway?" Jack suggested.

"How about your dad's place?"

"In Broadmoor?" Warily, her gaze darted to Jack, whose jaw tightened. He shifted toward Nina, giving her a bug-eyed, alarmed look. He mouthed the words *Your dad lived in Broadmoor?* and frowned.

"No, silly. BrightStar Assisted Living in Colorado Springs, where he lives now." Skylar paused. "You do know he lives there?"

Of course she did. "I do," she said solemnly, allowing a chunk of hair to come loose behind her ear and partially hide her face.

Jack shoved back his chair, scraping the floor. He shot up, stepped away from the table. From her. Hand on his temple, he glared at her.

Nina hurried through the details of when and where they'd meet. She hung up and turned to Jack.

"Jack," she pleaded, "I should have told you I lived in Broadmoor. I was young and honestly don't remember much."

He was pacing. Midstep, he stopped to look at her. "What about the bookstore?"

She shook her head. "I don't remember ever going there."

He rolled his eyes. He didn't believe her. Something unkind perched on his lips. She could see it in his intense stare, considering her with disdain. For some reason, he swallowed the words and began pacing.

"I don't remember, Jack," she said flatly.

"And your father?" He opened his mouth to say more and promptly shut it.

"I didn't lie, really." She was wringing her hands, considering what she should divulge. "I found him unconscious." Her voice softened. "Like I found Sam Wood." For so long, she had stamped down the details. Too painful. She squeezed her eyes shut.

"You had me believing that he'd passed."

"No," she insisted, slapping a hand on the table. "I never said he died."

"So he's alive?" Jack rifled a hand through his hair. "Why can't we ask him about Sam Wood? About the painting?" His voice rose. "About this whole damned mess you're in?" He huffed away, slamming the back door as he exited.

Nina felt under attack, and rightly so. It was time to tell him the truth.

# TWENTY-EIGHT

Jack stood a distance from the creek with his hands in his pockets. Nina inched up beside him, scuffed the dirt, not sure what to say. He didn't acknowledge her, and that was okay. She deserved his scorn. A dove moaned and pitched downward, following the creek bed and disappearing beyond the bend.

"Sorry, Jack." She searched for the bird. A dribble of water snaked through the creek. Enough to fill their silence with a faint gurgle.

She uncovered a stone with the toe of her shoe. She was stalling. Finally, she blew out a heavy breath and began.

"Every Thursday after work, I'd pop over to make sure my dad had eaten. I'd sift through his mail, water the plants, and spruce up the bathroom." She was staring across the creek at a thicket of pines. The simple tasks she enjoyed doing for him brought a smile. "The day I found him, I remember everything: the puffy clouds, a chill slipping inside my jacket. I stood at his door, knocking." She paused. "He never came." She sniffed away a tear.

"I found him in his recliner. Gaunt, head tilted back against the leather. He looked awkward, his mouth open, his chin pointed upward as if somehow that position brought air into his lungs. I called his name, softly at first. I kept yelling, 'Dad, wake up!' I grasped his hand, begged him to wake up." She paused, remembering the seconds that had passed, the panic rising in her throat. "I acted without thinking." A quick glance at Jack, wanting to know he was there, yet not wanting him to see the pain in her eyes. "I grabbed his ankles. With every bit of strength I could muster, I yanked him off the chair onto the rug and began CPR." Her lips twisted. She had more to say. But what was the point? "That's what happened," she said solemnly.

Jack, staring straight ahead, was slow to respond. "Sounds like you did the right thing."

Nina searched for the bird, wishing she could escape her memories, fly away, and forget her next admission. "The thing is, when his head hit the rug, it bounced." She bit her lip. "I damaged his brain, Jack." She shifted to him. "When I tugged him off the chair, I hurt him." The words stung, yet easily bubbled to the surface as if the admission brought a thread of relief. But it really didn't.

"Is that what the doctor said?" Jack finally looked at her, serious eyes searching hers.

"No." She shrugged. "They have no explanation why he can't speak or why he lays there staring out the window."

That wasn't exactly true. Brain-fuel deprivation was what they had called it. The more familiar name: hypoglycemia. Zero blood sugar. That was part of the problem. A double whammy with her antics, jerking him onto the floor. She lived with the depths of that action every day.

Now Jack hunched down, sifted a hand through the dirt. Finding a rock, he heaved it across the creek. "You can think that. But it's probably part of his condition." He looked at her and waited until their eyes met. "His condition isn't a reflection on you. Unless a medical doctor confirms your actions hurt him. You're not a doctor, Nina."

Jack sounded smug, or maybe that was the way she chose to hear it. She was holding on to her version. It made the most sense. And it explained why her father wouldn't look at her or change the disappointment set in his lifeless eyes.

*I was negligent.*

"I haven't been to visit him since Sam Wood died."

Jack stood. "Why?"

"Because I can't paint. My dad would be disappointed. He'd take one look at me and see what I did to him in my eyes." She ignored the pinch in her chest and thought of brighter, happier times. "I always talked to him about my painting. He gave me that gift, and it's our strongest bond." She turned to him. "He's the reason I paint, Jack."

"Painting isn't everything."

Nina didn't respond. It wouldn't make sense to him. *Because painting was her everything.*

Jack backpedaled. "Believe what you want. But that type of thing can destroy a person. Blame burns deep, and it's hard to wipe away."

"Like blaming yourself for Cam's . . ." She couldn't say it.

"Something like that." Jack's gaze landed on Nina and held, the edges of his eyes softening. He extended his hand and let out a sigh.

A quiet hung in the air. Finally, she reached for his hand. "A peace offering?"

"Let's just say we're fighting the same battle."

# TWENTY-NINE

Nina didn't sleep well. Visions of her father's tormented face filled her dreams. She awoke with a jolt. Someone was knocking at the front door.

Quickly shrugging on a robe and cursing her mother for habitually ignoring unsolicited visitors, Nina hurried to the door.

"Detective Kanoy."

He stood with hands behind his back, wearing that superior, closed-lip smile and rocking back on his heels. "You're looking . . . comfortable today, Nina."

"Thanks." It wasn't meant as a compliment. She forced a smile. That's what you did when a cop showed up at your door. *We're almost there,* he had said. Was this the moment she would be dragged away? She glanced back into Tisha's living room, a last freeze-frame snapshot, in case it was her last. She twisted back to face him. "What can I do for you?"

"I wanted to share a few developments. For one, we've received the autopsy report." He searched her eyes, tilted his head slightly as if expecting her to flinch.

Nina held a smile until her lips hurt.

Kanoy cleared his throat and withdrew a notepad from his shirt pocket. "Mr. Wood died from a lethal substance." He thumbed through the pages until he found what he wanted. "This wasn't an accidental or natural death. That much we know." He scratched behind an ear and leaned closer. "Do you mind if I come in? Neighbors might talk." He winked.

Nina wanted to slam the door in his face. "Sure, come in." Thoughts of sticking her foot out and tripping him crossed her mind. She opened the door wider and motioned toward the couch. Cinching the belt on her robe, she settled on the chair opposite the couch and crossed her legs. "If you don't mind me asking, what was the cause of death?"

He stared at her blankly as if she should have known the reason. He grumbled something before wetting a finger and flipping the page of the worn notepad. Resting into the cushions, he slung an arm across the back of the couch as if it were his couch, his house, and she, was the visitor. A long breath followed. "If I was to search the house, would I find turpentine?"

Nina shrugged. "This house?" She glanced around. "I have no idea, but I doubt it."

Kanoy grimaced. "I meant your house at 2304 Cimarron, Unit 2716."

Nina hadn't craved a drink in weeks, yet at this very moment, she wanted one. Badly. She swallowed, tasting her morning breath. "Of course I do." It was a ridiculous question. "I paint. Turpentine is used in oil painting, sometimes acrylic."

He glanced at his notepad and read verbatim: "Nina Shubert, a local artist in the Colorado Springs area, is known for her wet-on-wet watercolor technique. Her work examines quirky everyday subjects, and she paints them in a surprisingly new way. She was recently mentioned in *Artists Magazine* in their state-by-state Who's Who and Who to Watch sections." He looked up at her, expectant.

"Your point being I paint in watercolor. Not oil or acrylic?"

Kanoy stabbed his notepad with a spindly finger. "Exactly." Pleased with himself, he folded the notepad and tucked it back into his shirt pocket. "Cops are searching your place as we speak." Again, the closed-lip smile, bordering on creepy.

Nina held back a gasp. She wasn't going to let him see that she was rattled. Sucking in a breath, she laced her hands and spoke evenly. "You'll find turpentine, but that doesn't mean I killed Sam Wood. A lot of artists use paint thinners." *And if your detectives are good at their job, you'll find* Paris Beach *with Sam Wood's name on the back of the canvas. And if you searched this house, you'd find a sticky note most likely written by Sam Wood. There.* Her heart was pounding.

"But you were in Sam Wood's room, weren't you?"

Nina uncrossed her legs and leaned forward. "Again, that doesn't mean I killed him," she said evenly.

"Is that your official statement?" He rose, dug into his pockets, and pulled out keys.

She held his eyes, trying her best to appear unshaken by his accusations. "Yes, that's my statement."

Apparently in no hurry, he sauntered to the door. Just to torture her. He turned. "Want one?" He was holding a container of Tic Tacs.

Nina shook her head.

"One more thing." He popped a mint into his mouth. "Don't leave town."

When the door closed, Nina let out a heavy breath. The crunch of a crisp apple broke her reverie. Tisha sauntered into the room, palming said apple.

"Have you been eavesdropping, Mother?"

Eyes trained on the front door, Tisha took another bite. "Something like that."

Nina's eyes flickered up at her mother. "You could have defended me. Or at least stood beside me, showing your support." She knew that once they found the turpentine another dot would connect her. The final dot? Kanoy had warned her. She needed a lawyer. Bile rose to her throat. She wanted to puke.

"I'm sorry. I thought you handled it well." Tisha had a way of appearing nonplussed, almost gleeful when the conversation dictated otherwise. She took another bite, slowly chewing, still fixed on the door. "I was getting bad vibes from him."

"You think?" Nina wrung her hands.

"I've known from the start you didn't do it." Tisha lifted an eyebrow.

"And how is that, Mother?"

"I scattered aquamarine crystals around the house. For centuries, they've been touted as truth finders." Holding the core ends with her fingers, she nibbled the last bit. Chewing through her words, she said, "You're sitting on one now."

Nina lurched from the chair.

Tisha strutted over, dug a hand in the space between the cushion and chair, and plucked out a blue stone.

"You know I don't believe in that . . ." She wanted to say *crap*. A kinder word for her mother's little hobby wouldn't surface. Her glance fell to the stone. "Not exactly compelling evidence to share with the police." She rolled her eyes and walked away.

# THIRTY

Nina sat at a table facing the entrance to Santana's, an Italian casual dining restaurant. Jack had wanted to tag along. Nina had opted to come alone. Kanoy had spooked her. She hadn't told Jack about Kanoy coming to the house, afraid Jack would see it on her face. Her eyes, like her father's, were electric blue, serious, and reflective of every passing mood.

A cheery mural of immigrants gathered at a park flanked the wall across the room. Like Diego Rivera's style, there was much to see, much to distract her from meeting Skylar Whimpee . . . Whimpler. Something like that.

Nina gazed at the brightly colored painting. Usually, a bold fresco ripe with history held her interest. With bloodshot eyes from shoddy sleep and frazzled nerves, she couldn't hold focus. Her knee bounced nervously under the crisp, white tablecloth. All she could think about was Kanoy's pompous smile, his words. *Sam Wood died of a lethal substance.* She assumed turpentine.

For the umpteenth time, she shifted in the chair. She adjusted the book on the table: *Séance on a Summer's Night.* A random grab from Tisha's bookshelf as she had left the house. Skylar had gotten the idea from a movie to place a book on the table so she could easily spot Nina.

When Skylar entered, her eyes dipped to the book. One side of her mouth lifted. Not a full smile. More of a there-you-are smile. Wearing too-big sunglasses and loose, white linen pants and a jacket, she breezed up to the table, model-like in a forward hip stance. "Nina?" She removed the glasses. She looked to be in her mid-sixties with loose curls styled away from her face. "Nice to meet you," she said in the same breathy voice Nina had heard on the phone. But it was her eyes, sunken and dull, that surprised her.

Nina shifted to the book. "Good idea. Thanks."

"Your father bought books from me." Skylar gracefully slid in across from Nina, fluffed her hair with her fingers.

"What kind of books?"

"Rare books, mostly. That's how we met." Skylar smiled as if that thought sparked a memory. She pulled out a cigarette and held it between her fingers like a prop she somehow needed to continue. "He was quite a man, your father." She clasped her hands, holding the cigarette in shadow. The slightest uptick of her brow followed.

Nina wondered what that meant. She seemed too young to be her father's lover. Friends, maybe? Nina felt a tinge of jealousy. She shoved that down and got to the point. "Did my dad know Sam Wood?"

"I introduced them," she said proudly and fiddled with her prop.

A waiter dropped off menus and frowned at Skylar wielding the unlit cigarette. "Can't seem to stop." She shrugged and tucked the cigarette into the oversize pocket on her jacket. Ignoring the waiter, she addressed Nina. "Where were we?" She sighed. "Those two were like oil and water."

Nina prickled at the word *oil*. "How?"

"Your father was sensible, soft-spoken, generous, and I'd have to say naive at times. Sam tried hard to be a simple man without many wants." Skylar sipped the water the waiter had dropped off. "He turned greedy, and your father got in his way." She shivered, and her curls bounced about her face.

"How exactly?" Nina leaned in. "Does it have to do with *Paris Bench*?"

Upon hearing the name, Skylar's dull eyes flickered for half a second before returning to tired and narrow. "All I know is Sam Wood added his own special touches to *Paris Bench* and your father . . ." She searched for a word. "Took offense."

Nina felt like she'd been slapped. "My dad didn't paint *Paris Bench*?" She sat stunned. She must have misheard. "I don't understand?"

"Your father created the rudimentary shapes in lackluster colors. Sam made them come alive."

Skylar's words were matter-of-fact, like this sort of thing happened all the time. Nina didn't care for her descriptions of *rudimentary* or *lackluster*. That was not how her father painted. People who never painted were by far the biggest critics. Nina could almost let that slide. But artist copyright and overpainting? Nina clicked into defensive mode. She loved *Paris Bench*. Her father loved knowing she loved *Paris Beach*.

Disbelief clouded her thoughts. Her gut soured thinking of her father. Dealing with criticism. Defacing someone else's art was criminal. It took a moment to refocus on her reason for being there and formulate a question. "Is that what the blowup at the gallery was about?"

"Sam did something else." Skylar shrugged. "They were standing in front of the painting. The whole thing turned ugly. I'd never seen your father so mad. He looked like he'd pop a vein in his forehead."

Nina had never seen her father angry. A deep sigh and a brush across his bushy brows, yes. Maybe a stern arm-crossing. That was it. She had a hard time believing what Skylar was saying.

"It didn't help that they were center stage, lit beneath a spotlight for all to see. I didn't dare move closer." Skylar shook her head. "I never found out what caused the rift." She fingered the cigarette, started to pull it out, and decided against it. "Sam dumped me after that. I never got to see Paris, Egypt. Any of the places he'd promised to take me." She was biting her lip, hiding any further hint of dissatisfaction with her eyes cast downward. "I even bought my ticket." She brightened. "Lent him money to buy his." She tried to appear unphased, but her lips were quivering. "One day, he drops a shiny stone in my hand, tells me he's sorry for everything."

"A stone or a crystal?" Nina looked surprised.

"I wouldn't know the difference. Jasper or something like that."

"A stone."

"I tossed it." A loose curl fell across her face, and she tucked it behind her ear. "After me, he dated another girl at the bookstore, I think, before he met Odilia." Skylar sighed. "Rumors spread about him being a ladies' man."

She stared off at nothing, and Nina let her have that moment before asking, "Who would know about that night at the gallery?" There had to be someone.

"His wife?" Skylar tossed out. "Sam had something burning inside him. He seemed quiet, but I never liked the way he was always searching for something better." She frowned. "The pisser is, he really liked your dad. Even more than me. He blew off a date and visited your dad instead." Skylar picked up the book and lazily flipped through the pages. "Your dad sure loves books. I read to him when I visit. We travel to all sorts of places on those pages." She looked up at Nina, her eyes twinkling. "I thought you should know about the gallery incident. I figured if you did the deed, I'd never hear from you. Boy . . ." she hesitated, shaking her head in disbelief. "Someone murdering Sam Wood." She mulled over the words.

"I could have pulled the trigger after the way Sam Wood treated me. I lost my job because of him. The owner of the bookstore accused me of stealing books. A few of her special orders." Skylar glared off in the distance. "I knew it was him." Her gaze snapped back to Nina. "Sam stole the books," she said sharply. Then, as if she could forgive him, given the chance, she waved away the thought. "I never found my way after him." She pursed her lips, posed seductively with her head held at an angle, giving Nina a glimpse of the starlet she once was. Bright, playful eyes. Pouty lips. "I was a catch back then." She chuckled until she realized Nina wasn't. "You know I'm joking about Sam? I didn't kill him."

"I know," Nina said. "Sam didn't die from a bullet."

Skylar snapped the book closed, an odd smile on her lips. A knowing smile that wasn't supposed to seep out. Nina knew that because Skylar immediately tucked her lips together, removing any trace. But Nina had caught it and wondered what she was thinking at that moment. Could she have written the note? It seemed unlikely. But there was something about Skylar. Something Nina couldn't quite pin down.

Skylar pushed away from the table. But Nina had one more question. "Can you tell me about the painting in the nook?"

"I thought I'd get to Paris one day. When that dream faded, I had one of the employees replicate what I remembered of *Paris Bench* but in a way children would enjoy."

Nina smiled, warming up to the painting, yet still troubled by the nook. One more question. "When I lived in Broadmoor as a child, did you ever see me at the bookstore?"

Skylar shook her head. "Not on my watch."

# THIRTY-ONE

N ina smiled at Bob Dylan gliding along the craggy rocks in the tank. She hadn't killed the fish. That was something. Her mind was stuck on the story in the morning's paper.

*Catching Up with the Caspian Killer*

*According to a source at the El Paso County Coroner's Office, a substance was identified as the cause of death for Mr. Samuel Wood, who was staying at the Caspian Hotel on September 12. While the police continue to question the woman who was in the room at the time Mr. Wood was found deceased, the Caspian Killer's name has yet to be released.*

What a crock.

She handed the paper to Jack to read while she continued to spy on Bob Dylan. So far, Faith Hill had remained in the hollowed log on the opposite end of the tank. She didn't trust Bob Dylan. Nina was sure of it.

Jack folded the paper. "At least your name has been kept out of the media."

It seemed a small win. Her connecting-the-dots theory and Kanoy's biting words turned her stomach. She collapsed into the chair beside Jack.

She liked it here at The Fishing Hole. Jack's optimism shone just when she needed it. This was one of those moments. He tossed her a bag of SunChips.

Nina told him about her meeting with Skylar. Jack scratched his head. "Sam painted over *Paris Bench*. Huh." He dug into his bag of chips.

"And he did *something else*." Nina made air quotes. "Skylar didn't elaborate." Nina still couldn't believe it. How could her father, the legend behind the creation, have lied about the painting? She knew parents did that. A white lie for the betterment of the child. Nina couldn't see her father doing that and preferred to deny all that Skylar had said.

Nina's thoughts drifted to the crystal. She turned to Jack. "The jasper crystal rings too close to home."

Jack split open the bag of chips. "Could Sam have also known your mom?"

Nina shook her head. "Tisha would have told me. Sam's name has been tossed around too much for her not to slip it in. Remember, she's the crystal queen. If Sam had been feeding into her hocus-pocus, she'd be gloating."

Jack slipped a chip in his mouth, chewed thoughtfully. "Did you see a crystal in his hotel room that day?"

"No," she said flatly. "I was focused on him, hoping he'd wake up. What was or wasn't in the room never crossed my mind. Besides, they found the crystal in his pocket." She was biting her nail. "Could someone have slipped it in there?"

"It's plausible. Maybe we need to go back to the—"

Before he finished the sentence, Nina was shaking her head. "No, I can't go back to the Caspian."

"I'll be with you every step."

Her eyes trailed away from him.

"We'll hold hands."

He was being cute. This wasn't the time for cute, yet a tiny smile surfaced.

"Maybe being there will stir up a memory."

She thought about the bee boxes. She was seven, scouting around the backyard beyond the fence. A stack of shelves had caught her attention. Ever curious, she had opened one. Within seconds, an angry swarm gathered. She took off running, and they followed, taking turns stinging her head. Her father, sitting on the porch, shooed them away. With the patience of Job, he pulled the stingers from her scalp while telling her about a famous Renaissance painting. Cupid and bees. Something like that. She hardly cried. Later, the welts throbbed like the stingers were still embedded. Even now when her hair swirled in the wind, she looked around for bees. Going to the Caspian was like visiting those bee stings. She didn't want to stir up the pain.

She shifted to the fish. Bob Dylan appeared orange today with flecks of gold. She breathed heavily, crossed her arms. She wasn't used to being swayed so easily. She didn't want to return to the Caspian. Watching the fish, she gritted her teeth. Then she looked at Jack, about to tell him no, she wouldn't go. His face turned serious yet a twinkle danced in his eyes. The fear of going somehow crumbled. At least enough for her to reconsider. "When can we go?"

# THIRTY-TWO

S oft jazz and low chatter filled the bar at the Caspian. Apparently, the bar had a name. Penrose Pub. Nina had missed the sign behind the bar, lost among the shelves of colorful booze bottles.

No empty tables. At the bar, one stool sat empty. They opted to wait for a table. Nina spent the time casing the layout, seeing it through fresh eyes. A marble bar top. Twelve or so dining tables. Windows leading out to the pool area banked one wall. Jack, leaning against a post, scanned the room. Nina stared at him realizing that, to him, this was just a bar with light eats, like any bar filled with the hum of conversation and whiffs of garlic and grilling meat.

Jack lifted his chin. His eyes trailed to a table where a foursome argued over who paid what. Finally, an older fellow stood and slapped bills on the table, and they left. Jack swooped in.

"Is this what you remember?" Jack scooted in her chair and sat beside her.

Nina glanced around. "The same, I guess, but with people."

The bar oozed energy. Before, it had read like after hours, raw and quiet, hiding secrets. In her mind, she had considered her time at the bar as a precursor to a crime. A shadowy place where she shouldn't have been lurking. Like a dark alleyway leading toward danger. Seeing it alive muddled her memories.

"A drink?" Jack turned over the menu, searching out the beverages.

"Not a chance." She couldn't believe he suggested a drink. Not after what had happened the last time she had swilled whiskey at this bar. She shuddered. "Water for me." When the cute waitress with the high ponytail moseyed over, he ordered two Perriers.

Jack spread his legs and angled toward the bar. "You sat at the far right?"

Her insides twisted. "And Stuart sat to the left," she whispered.

Jack pointed. "And that's the hallway."

She nodded. "The creepy one without much light and an angry ice machine." A heaviness settled over her shoulders. A reminder of her involvement in Sam Wood's death. Could she have helped him? *I should have called 911, attempted CPR.* She slumped lower in the chair. With the rise in her heartbeat, she regretted coming. "Jack . . ."

He reached out a hand, a gesture she appreciated but didn't re-ciprocate. "When you're ready. Not a moment sooner."

"I'm not sure," she said quietly. Could she go down that hallway? She bit her thumbnail, eyeing the shadowy entrance, then her gaze darted back to the bar, to the stool where she had sat and where the sad man had roosted close by. She pictured Stuart there, hunched and foreboding, hiding something in the bulk of his winter garb. Or just trying to hide himself. It had to be him. That conviction stirred something inside her. The room seemed to tilt a fraction, sliding pieces together. The skittering in her chest calmed.

"Maybe Stuart wasn't wearing a knitted cap with flaps." A glimpse of his profile flashed behind her eyes. Double chin resting on his shirt. Something on his ears. Not a cap with earflaps.

"Headphones, not earflaps," she said a little too loud, and heads turned. She leaned in and whispered, "Jack, he had on headphones." She thought a moment. "And a hat. Not a winter hat. More of a beanie. Red."

"Beanies can be knitted."

"I guess. I don't remember." She closed her eyes and plunged back into that night. A clink of a glass. The hum of a distant vacuum. Stuart thumping the bar top. And her leg was bouncing. The thrill of the award. Bursting energy with nowhere to go.

Another recollection surfaced. Her eyes flashed open. She looked at Jack. "My heel slipped off the rung." She frowned, looked down as if it had just happened. *Then what?* "He'd shoved away from the bar, the barstool scraping the floor. I think he kicked out his foot or something. I remember someone, maybe, hidden in the hallway, reaching out to grab…"

"What?"

Stuart, the bulk of him flashed in her mind. And the faint edges of another person.

"Nina, that doesn't make sense. This is a bar." Jack's expression bordered on frustration. "What would he be kicking? And to who? You said there was no one else here."

She tossed up her hands. "Your guess is as good as mine." She tapped the water bottle, channeling Stuart. Nothing. She plodded back to Stuart's barstool and pivoted to face the hall from that vantage point. In slow motion, she lifted her foot in a mock kick. The woman seated in Stuart's chair harrumphed before turning her back to Nina.

Nina shrugged. She was contemplating possibilities, retracing her steps, trying to decipher a scenario that made sense. Again, she paced toward the dimly lit hall, stopping short as if on an imaginary line. Once she slipped into the darkness, there was no turning back. She sensed Jack beside her, his silent support a physical force propping her upright.

"Nothing?"

She turned to him. He looked like the way she felt. Defeated. She sighed. It was time. Reaching for Jack's hand, she squeezed it and planted her feet beneath her. Then, taking a step forward, she left the incandescent light of the bar and entered a place where her world had become dark.

# THIRTY-THREE

I ce machines should have a silent mode. Or at least a warning. Like the day she had found Sam Wood down this very hall, Nina jumped when the machine churned. Jack's free hand grasped her arm. A calming touch, urging her to continue. They'd wandered farther along the quiet hall.

"I think I stopped here." Ahead, the hallway curved right. Nina's pulse quickened as a shaky hand pointed. "Just down there." Each step counted off an imaginary alarm. As if she could somehow calm the thrumming, she laid a palm on her chest. "I saw the girl there." Nina imagined the large, almond-shaped eyes, fingers dipping into her mouth. "I think she was afraid, Jack."

"Could she have been the person in the hall?"

Nina shrugged. A part of her wanted to believe that and keep thinking about the girl instead of shifting to the other side of the hall where she had found Sam. In *that* room, she could have done something. A big something that she couldn't remember. Would it come flooding back? Part of her wished she could cry, slough off the raw edges of what she was feeling. The truth, whatever it may be, could swallow her whole, and there would be no coming back.

She stood taller, sucked in a breath.

*You can do this.*

She slowly turned, lifted her eyes to the door.

Nothing. No "aha" moment. She sighed. Anticipation unraveled like a fuse snuffed out in the nick of time. It was just a door, albeit paint-chipped. Just a standard hotel door where someone else would happily sleep tonight and shower in the morning. No electrodes beeping. No case of wonder drugs. No trace of Sam Wood. She had expected a jolt, a rush of terror, crumpling into the fetal position. Was it wrong to be disappointed? She walked over and thoughtfully rested a hand on the wooden veneer, feeling the tiny grooves beneath her fingertips. A shiver slipped down her spine. A part of her wanted to go inside, stare down the chair and face the final minutes when the blip on the monitor had flatlined.

*Sam, what happened to you?*

Realizing someone could be inside, she stepped away. She'd lost herself in the room, slipping under the door to watch Sam sit limply in the chair, will him to tell her what had happened. A whisper of words. The last words on his lips making the perfect O.

Jack, now down the hall, called out, "I found a door that leads to the pool area." He pushed on the lever. A crack of light washed over him, and he squinted. "Someone could have slipped out this way, circled around." With a thud, the door closed.

"Stuart?" she asked.

A man hauling a snowboard clumped by. Jack smiled, waited until he passed. "Maybe." He joined her. "What about the girl and her mother? Did the police interview them?"

"I don't know."

"I wonder if we could find out their names. They had to have seen something before you entered the room."

She liked that he believed her, even if at that very moment she doubted herself.

———————

The check-in desk was deserted. An orchestral, cheery tune serenaded them as they waited for the slight woman with a thoughtful smile tucking fall leaves along the counter.

"Checking in?" She abandoned the project and walked over to the computer.

Jack smiled. "Actually, we were wondering if you could give us a guest name on a specific date a few months back."

With that smile, Nina would have turned over Social Security numbers. This woman frowned. "We can't do that. Privacy laws. We could be sued."

"The thing is," Jack said, "it could help resolve an incident that happened here. We're just trying to flesh out a few leads." He held up a hand. "No addresses. No phone numbers. Just a name."

A hard no didn't follow. That was a good sign, and the two of them waited her out, appearing hopeful with wide smiles. Finally, she picked up a card, slid it toward them. "We get points for positive reviews." She motioned with a flick of her hand. "Make me proud." She winked.

While Nina wrote a glowing statement about Beth (per her name tag) and the Caspian, Jack supplied the few specifics they had. Beth poked around the corner toward a door marked *Private* before pecking at the keyboard. She scribbled on a piece of paper. "I remember those folks. Received complaints about the little girl disturbing guests with a soccer ball in the hallway." She dropped an assortment of Hershey's miniatures on top of the paper. "Leftovers from Halloween," she explained. "No Krackels, though. My grandson likes those." She returned to the fall leaves.

Jack tugged at Nina's hand. A quick walk through the lobby and they exited the hotel. Jack unfolded the paper. "Caroline Warner." He held up a hand, expected a high-five.

Nina made the motion, but her mind was turning. "This means Stuart was involved. Caroline's his wife. And this explains the girl in the hallway. She had a ball, Jack." She snatched the paper from Jack's hand. "It can't be a coincidence that they were in the room across from Sam."

"I agree." Jack rifled a hand through his hair, glanced around, searching. "I'm hungry. You?"

She wasn't, but she didn't want her time with Jack to end. The pieces were falling together. Progress. Yet something felt brittle. Being on the cusp of discovering the truth made her uneasy. "Can we go somewhere?" She looked over her shoulder. "Away from here."

"I know a place."

On the edge of The Galleries, they settled on a bench skirting a slope of grass abutting the shops. A string of lights outlined the roof of a hot dog stand parked along the sidewalk. After hours, a handful of food trucks tucked along the street. People strolled The Gallery grounds, which were lit until midnight. The well-tended tropical landscape drew joggers and lovers.

Nina nuzzled up to Jack. "It's time to tell Kanoy." She tucked a hand into the pocket. "He'll need to know about my dad and what happened to him. Otherwise, it won't make sense how I found Sam." That thought was sobering. She swallowed, willing the guilt to stay away. It had a way of filling her chest. "And Odilia. I've stalled long enough." As much as she didn't want to see her, Nina had to know. The missing piece was still out there. "I need to know what happened at the Crescent Moon Gallery."

"*We,*" he emphasized. "We have to visit Odilia."

They remained silent for a time. Light settled behind a clump of trees in the distance. A swirl of orange backlighting bare branches. A dribble of patrons lined up for a warm dog and something sweet. Nina sniffed the hypnotic sweetness.

"What do you know about Odilia Wood?" Jack asked.

A whiff of caramel corn floated in the breeze. Despite the heady sugar smell, Nina frowned. "Odilia's not friendly. At least, not to me. Then again, I ran into her at her husband's memorial." Nina crossed her legs toward Jack, wanting to be closer, warmer. "She insinuated I was drinking with Sam in his hotel room, and I'm sure she thought . . . more happened." She didn't want to think about Odilia. The day had caught up with her. The Caspian had proved too much. Tired, she wanted to go home.

A car passed. A black sedan, one of those newer models with headlights that wrapped around the side of the car, like evil cat eyes. "I passed out at the bookstore." Her eyes followed the car around the corner until it disappeared. "Could I have passed out in Sam's hotel room? What if I did something horrible?" She didn't want to believe that she was capable of something like that. How could she discount it, though? That was the problem with creative folks. Imagination was her superpower.

Jack fished out his wallet. "I don't know. Seems pretty far-fetched to me. Why would you have wanted to hurt him? You didn't know about *Paris Bench* then. Is that motive for murder?" He pulled out cash and tucked his wallet away.

The same car passed again. Jack stood. "Mustard and relish on your dog?"

She was watching the car limp past them.

"Nina?"

She tore her gaze away from the car. "Sure. Mustard, relish," she said offhandedly.

Jack gave her that look, searching her face for an explanation. A shrug morphed into a shiver. He shook his head. "What was I thinking?" He shrugged off his jacket. "You look freezing." He tucked it around her like a blanket, the fur ruffling under her chin. Adjusting the edges, a warm hand grazed her cheek. She wanted to lean into his touch, but he pulled away. "Let's pay Odilia a visit."

Nina frowned. "She won't be happy to see me."

"Let's bring flowers. Who doesn't love a bouquet?" Usually, his craggy and worn smile lifted her out of her funk. But seeing Odilia and being peppered with accusations again was the last thing Nina wanted. Yet she had to. Odilia was her last hope of finding out what had happened between Sam and her father at Crescent Moon Gallery.

While Jack sauntered off for hot dogs, Nina shuffled around the idea of visiting Odilia. Somehow the dread softened in knowing Jack would be there. Still, Odilia worried Nina. The way her eyes had jerked away that day at the church. She had lashed out at Nina, all but accusing her of sleeping with her husband. Despair could crumble a person. Yet Nina sensed something deeper, something sinister in Odilia's sneer and sharp tone. Then again, Nina had never lost someone in the true sense of the word. A cool gust snuck inside Jack's jacket. She shivered, tucked her chin into the fur.

Jack returned and placed the dogs between them. She tossed a glance at the street, searching for that same car. She was hoping not to see it and let go of the breath she was holding. A wash of light illuminated the empty street. Only people milling about. No cars.

Jack untwisted the bag of caramel corn and grabbed a handful. He managed to stuff it all in his mouth.

Nina plucked a kernel and sucked off the salty goodness before chewing.

They were both staring at the street. The weight of being close to answers, close to Kanoy hauling her in, close to the end of everything she had known, heightened her senses. She needed to think straight.

"So, what don't we know?" Sam asked.

"The turpentine. How did it enter Sam's system? Was it ingested?"

Jack stole a sliver of the coat and curled toward her, resting an arm across the back of the bench. He rifled through the bag. "Did the police find *Park Bench* at your condo?"

"Would they arrest me for having Sam's painting?"

"No. The painting gives your dad motive. Not you."

"What about me?" She turned to Jack, searched his eyes.

"What about you?" Jack countered.

"Could someone have wanted me to be found in Sam's room?"

"A setup?"

She was close enough to feel his warm, sugary breath skate across her cheek. She pulled back, focused on the possibility of a setup. "Who? Skylar? No." Nina shook her head. "It had to be art-related."

"Or related to your father? *Park Bench?*" Jack, considering the possibility, lifted a kernel to his lips. "Before Odilia, you need to visit your dad."

A wistful thought of her father formed until head beams flashed on. Two tunnels of light brightened the street in front of them. The rub of tires slowly passing by, the vehicle a dark color, maybe an SUV. The same evil cat eyes.

# THIRTY-FOUR

Nina had chosen BrightStar Assisted Living because of the art. Of course, she had vetted the facility, the doctors, and had read Yelp comments. But it was the lobby where *The Starry Night*, *Girl with a Pearl Earring*, and *Whistler's Mother* hung that had swung the pendulum in BrightStar's favor.

How naive she'd been to think her father would slip into the hall at night and sink into one of the cozy chairs to admire the paintings. Seeing them now—replicas in gaudy, gilded frames—flipped a switch inside her. A familiar high she swam in whenever she dove into the art world. It could be a picture in a magazine, a postcard she'd received, or a child's finger painting on someone's fridge. It didn't matter. She loved paintings. Period. She sighed. It was still hard to reconcile that Sam Wood had doctored her father's painting. A painting she adored. It was more than that, really. That painting had breathed life into her purpose.

Nina strolled down the hall. A faint odor of disinfectant tickled her nose. Above, fluorescent lights, stark and beyond bright. Clinical white walls with official signs pointing staff and visitors toward exits and meeting rooms. All reminders that her father no longer watched *Dateline* in his favorite recliner.

Skylar had graced these halls while Nina had stayed away. A lump formed in her throat. She'd abandoned her father. She knew that now.

Shame mixed with excitement met her at the door of Room 124. She sucked in a breath, stood tall, and walked inside.

"Dad," she said brightly and bent to kiss his hollowed cheek. Always a thin man, his skin appeared almost translucent, exposing every bone. Especially in his face. The hard angles on his cheekbones, brow, and chin, half-lit by light streaming in from the window. They'd moved his bed closer to the sunlight. Maybe that was why his face listed toward the window. Whatever the reason, she smiled. She missed him. All her reasons for staying away vanished. She had been selfish, thought she saw disappointment in his face. *She* was projecting her own disappointment onto him. That was a thing, wasn't it? Her eyes stung, but no tears came.

How could she have stayed away? Now, seeing him changed everything. Getting caught up in losing her Best of Show status paled in comparison. Being here with him, she realized, was what mattered.

"I miss you." She kissed his hand, all knuckles and blue veins. Dribble glistened below his lips. She wiped it away and sought his eyes. They didn't waver from their pained, distant stare. "I have so much to tell you," she said in a whisper. All she could muster without spilling tears.

Nina dragged a chair beside the bed. She reached for the remote, turned off the TV. She curled an arm under his and held his hand. Stroking his arm, she unwound the last month like a tight ball tethered in her chest. Really, she was talking to herself, and that was fine.

She rattled on about finding Sam Wood in the hotel room, about being unable to paint, about Jack, and meeting Skylar and how lucky he was to have her visit.

A lamp on the table beside the bed flashed on. She hadn't realized how long she'd sat there. Like one of her visits to his home, she had gabbed on far too long. He always listened. But was he today?

A tiny woman with shiny, black hair pulled into a tight bun strolled in. "You feed him today?" She held out a tray.

Nina, looking at her father, hesitated before finally nodding. She had missed so much time with him. With the help of the aide, they maneuvered the table over the bed. She listened to the do's and don'ts of feeding a nonambulatory patient. The aide pointed to the containers. "Creamed chicken, creamed carrots, apple juice. Good stuff for a strong man." The tiny woman lifted on her toes and leaned over the bed railing. "Eat up, Mr. Shubert." She gave a bright smile and left.

Nina grimaced at the tray. She picked up the baby spoon and dipped it in the chicken.

"We have a plan, Jack and I." She lifted the spoon to her father's lips. "We need to find out how the turpentine entered Sam's body." He barely opened his mouth. "I imagine it tastes awful." She backtracked. "I mean the turpentine. Maybe someone mixed it in his food or a drink?" She waited. Eventually, her father's jaw started working. And his Adam's apple moved, registering a swallow. "Great, Dad."

The carrots looked disgusting. She stirred the concoction as if that somehow helped. "Did I tell you *Paris Bench* is at my condo?" She raised the spoon to his lips. "Come on, Dad. Just a few more bites."

His jaw clenched, contorting his entire face into a red-tinged scowl. This surprised Nina. She hadn't known he could move that way. Nina rested back in the chair. "I know it stings, even now, knowing Sam ruined your painting." She set the spoon on the tray and lifted the carton. "Juice?" The hard edge of his jaw twitched. "Okay." She held up a hand. "No juice."

She slid the table away. Enough feeding for now. "Good news." She brightened. "We're talking to Odilia tomorrow. Hopefully, she can shed light on—"

His hand shot up in the air and, with a thud, slapped the bedsheet.

# THIRTY-FIVE

"Something isn't right, Jack." The water was running in the sink in the back office. She'd spilled ketchup on her blouse, just below her neckline. She dabbed at the cotton print. "So clumsy," she muttered under her breath.

She felt off since seeing her father's reaction. The aide had asked her to leave after Nina questioned the woman about his movements. Why hadn't she asked before how he was doing? Obviously, he had improved to some degree. A tad violent in her mind, but still an improvement. Feeling shaky and plain out of sorts, Nina didn't want to visit Odilia today.

"We should go, Nina. Your dad was trying to tell you something. You know, a sign." Jack ate the last few fries.

"I don't believe in signs, remember?" Nina turned off the tap.

Her cell phone chimed. Grabbing a napkin off the counter, she wiped her hands before plucking the phone from her pocket. It was Kanoy. She put the call on speaker.

"Someone named Jack called me on your behalf?"

"Yes." Jack stepped closer to the counter where the phone sat. "We . . . I should say, Nina wanted to know how the turpentine entered Mr. Wood's system."

Kanoy harrumphed. They could hear papers shuffling. "Syringe," he said dryly. "Your standard hypodermic needle, most likely. They found a pinpoint injection site between his toes. Addicts do that." He paused. "Sam Wood didn't present with drugs in his system, and according to his wife, he never took illegal drugs. You?"

Nina rolled her eyes at Jack. "Of course not. I wouldn't even know how to use a needle."

"Now that we have a murder weapon, we're making the rounds."

Nina, eyebrows drawn together, looked at Jack. "What does that mean?" Jack shrugged.

"Searching Sam Wood's home, the hotel, your residence, The Art Loft gallery."

"The Art Loft?" Nina's eyes darted about the room. Still gripping the edge of her blouse, she realized she'd loosened the top button. A slight shift of her hand and the delicate pearl button fell, rolling under the counter.

"We have to be thorough," Kanoy explained.

Nina panicked.

Searching her house again, she understood. But where she worked? It felt like an invasion, and honestly, she didn't want to involve Stacey. She already felt put out by the press harassing the gallery.

Jack had ducked down, searching for the button. Nina offered Kanoy a short goodbye and hung up the phone. She didn't care about the button or being polite to Kanoy. "I have to see Stacey."

"Then Odilia's?"

"Maybe." Nina couldn't think beyond a face-to-face with Stacey before the police got to her.

—————————

They were too late. Two lanky police officers were exiting The Art Loft, taking the concrete stairway by two between the buildings leading to the street.

Nina hurried across the street, leaving Jack behind. The older cop, balding with a thick mustache, glanced at Nina edging the steps, as far as possible away, doing her best to appear invisible. When they passed, she barely met their eyes and smiled.

Inside, Nina caught her breath. She waited for Jack to summit the stairs. Maybe she was panicking for no reason. There was nothing to find. Yet she was doubting herself again. Jack entered, slightly winded. She craned her head over his shoulder, not wanting to turn around. "Are they gone?"

Jack nodded. "So, this is where you work?"

Nina didn't reply and began searching for Stacey, ducking into the partitioned spaces throughout the gallery that displayed various artists. She found her in the warehouse on the floor, holding a screwdriver and surrounded by two-by-fours.

Stacey looked up, surprised at first, then smiled. "Just in time. Have you ever made a shelf from scratch?" Without waiting for an answer, she abandoned the project, sprang up like a nimble gymnast, and pranced into the showroom. "Looked way easier on YouTube." Slipping a bent leg under her, she cozied into the chair behind her desk and snatched a pen. "I'm guessing you're here about the visitors?"

Nina crossed her arms.

"They were looking for a syringe," Stacey explained. "Wanting to know if I'd found one or any evidence of a syringe on the premises."

"I hope you told them no."

Jack snuck in behind Nina and waved. "Hi. I'm Jack."

Stacey gave him a who-are-you look.

"He's with me," Nina explained curtly. She focused on Stacey. Nina wanted to hear the words from her mouth. *No, Officers. I didn't find a syringe.* "Well?" She waited.

Stacey swiveled a half turn before returning to face the desk. "Did you hear Sarah's pregnant?"

Nina tried to smile. "Great. What about the syringe?"

"With in vitro, she had to give herself shots. She must have done that here." Stacey tightened her ponytail, unwilling to look at Nina. "I found a hypodermic needle in the trash. I told her she needed to—"

Nina didn't care. "When did you find the needle?"

"I told the cops it was a Tuesday last month. I remember because it was street-sweeping day and I wanted to get the needle out of the bathroom trash and out to the curb bin before the trash truck came. Easy to remember. Street sweepers come the same day."

Jack turned to Nina. "When did Sam die?"

"Last month."

"You were in last month." Stacey was speaking slowly, now seeking out Nina's eyes. "Your last day? Remember?"

Fear washed over Nina. She twisted away, stared at a charcoal drawing. Brooding clouds during a wildfire. One blackened and brittle tree stood against the angry sky. "I got a parking ticket outside the gallery on that day. Street-sweeping day."

# THIRTY-SIX

Sitting beside Jack in the pickup, Nina trembled. Clasping her hands between her legs, she tried to think of anything other than the damned needle. *I didn't do it,* she kept telling herself. The engine sputtered and she jumped. Jack pumped the gas and swung the wheel, heading down a side street. A few blocks away, he parked.

"Why can't I remember exactly what happened in Sam's hotel room that day?" She didn't want to remember a needle in her hand. *God, don't let me remember a needle.*

Jack dropped his hands from the wheel. "You told me what happened pretty clearly when you stopped by for an eye exam." He made air quotes when he said "eye exam," no doubt trying to add levity. But there was no calming her. And his smile wasn't amusing either.

"I could never give someone a shot between the toes. In the arm. Anywhere." In no scenario would that happen.

"I believe you." He touched her knee. A quick touch.

"You're the only one." She sank deeper into the seat, feeling the ripped pleather against her back and somehow liking the way it scratched her spine.

"And your mother," he added. "She believes you. Remember the aquamarine crystals?"

"Truth finders." Nina rolled her eyes. Suddenly, tears stained her face. She sniffled. "I never cry," she said, almost laughing.

"Apparently you do." He reached over her and fished a wrinkled fast-food napkin out of the glove box.

She dabbed her eyes. "Life used to be so simple: paint, submit my work, repeat."

"Sounds monotonous."

"Not the painting part. Well, maybe a little with my hypervigilance about getting a Best of Show designation. But this?" She slowly nodded in frustration.

"What did you think would happen once you got the title?"

It was chilly, and she shivered, her shoulders folding in. "I had it for a split second." She mused before turning serious. "The title would give me credibility. My art would sell."

"Those two aren't mutually exclusive."

"My chances improve. And my dad." She paused. "He'd be so proud." His smile meant the world to her. They didn't look alike, father and daughter. She had her mother's thick mop of hair, her full lips, and olive skin. Her father had given her his temperament and his book seriousness. "He taught me that practice and following a plan were equally important to my achievement, whatever that might be." She shifted to Jack, who was looking at her expectantly, as if what she had said hadn't been enough or had been shallow. "I've done all the right things, Jack. Next in line was Best of Show. *Credibility.*" She emphasized the word, but he didn't get it and shrugged. "My dad's eyes lit up when we talked about art. Sparks flew between us like we were speaking our own language."

"I get that. But I think if you never painted again, your dad would still be proud of you." When she didn't respond, he continued. "Cam didn't have to do anything special, and I was proud of him." Jack's baby blues turned serious. "I'd give anything to tell him that."

How could she argue with that? She remained quiet, letting his words sink in. Self-doubt was hard to cast off. Without the Best of Show, she felt cheated, unsure where to go from there. Everyone needed someone in their corner to rally them through tough times. For so long, it had been her father.

If Jack had wanted to distract her with talk about her art, it had run its course. The weight of the new evidence about the needle settled back inside her chest. A dull ache. The heaviness stole her breath. She felt broken and didn't know how much more she could endure. They were out of leads. It was happening . . . a spiral from which she couldn't recover.

She shifted to Jack. "What comes after Odilia? What if this never goes away, Jack?"

"Something will come up. Things change, Nina. They always do." He scratched the whiskers that had formed along his jawline.

"That's what I'm afraid of."

# THIRTY-SEVEN

The pixie of a woman manning the front desk at BrightStar appeared alarmed when she checked Nina in via the computer. Her fake lashes briefly fluttered up to Nina before she ducked down and whispered into the intercom system. A stodgy woman wearing a proper pantsuit arrived, and the two conversed out of earshot. The higher-up pulled Nina aside. In a polite sort of way, she read from her handheld device.

"The notes claim you agitated the patient and are potentially harmful to his recovery." She averted her eyes, watching a man with a walker clomp by at a snail's pace.

"Yes, my father was agitated," Nina agreed. "I see his agitation, as well as any movement, as an improvement to his nonverbal state. Possibly the therapist can work at refining those movements." She smiled, holding it a tad too long. "We all want the same thing: Dad to be better." Nina touched the woman's arm, something that used to feel awkward and intrusive.

The nurse's shoulders loosened. It took a moment of hemming and hawing before she smiled. "Go on ahead." Her focus fell to the handheld. "I'll rework the notes."

Sometimes a girl just needed her father. Nina felt that way this morning. Her paths were narrowing. Kanoy wanted to see her again. His team had confiscated *Paris Bench*. They knew about Sam Wood's name on the canvas. Just the thought of the painting in police custody made Nina's scalp prickle. She hadn't responded to Kanoy's voice mail and wondered if that made her appear guilty. She sighed and followed along the hallway, bypassing the masterpieces in the lounge altogether. She couldn't endure the ache, seeing those paintings again. Hopelessness weighed her down, each step drudgery. Yet she had rallied a convincing spiel for the nurse. That was a win.

When she entered her father's room, everything looked the same. What had she expected? Maybe a slight incline to the bed so he could see above the hedges, onto the street. He loved people watching and shared it with her. She wanted to think he was doing that now and somehow laughing on the inside.

"Hi, Dad." Nina glanced at the tray on the table saddling the bed. Apple juice with a straw. An opened but untouched chocolate pudding. A pile of napkins. Nina went to slide the contraption away from the bed. Something rolled out from under the napkins. It was a crystal.

"Huh." Nina picked it up, twirled it in her fingers. Lavender with striations.

She looked at her father, wishing he could tell her who had put it there. He blinked. Not unusual. He blinked again. When his eyelids rose, his irises, gray and distant, tracked toward her.

"Dad?" she said more like a question. She scooted around the bed to his line of sight and held the stone in her palm. "I wish you could tell me who left this." Her eyes bore into his, hoping to see movement. His glance had returned to the window, his eyes fixed. It was worth a try. "Go back to people watching, Dad."

A chair sat beside the bed. She wondered if Skylar had stopped by. Or someone else. But who? Nina sat and began her usual upbeat chitchat. After the last time, she stayed away from the case. Art, the obvious commonality, flowed out of her. If only she could cocoon herself here and forget the last few months. Maybe she could forgive herself for what happened to him. She rarely veered from the staunch viewpoint that she was indeed the perpetrator of his injury.

She shifted to him. The contours of his face didn't appear as harsh or drawn. He was simply an old man who'd suffered a brain injury. That's all. Optimism brightened her thoughts. She dared to have hope. If only for a brief moment.

Perhaps she could convince herself the nightmare would end. She didn't need an alibi. True, she was there, but Sam had already passed. It was a matter of motive, and she had none. She hadn't allowed these ideas to surface. She thought the worst instead. A lightness fluttered inside her, and for a thin minute, she considered rushing home and painting.

Footfalls sounded at the door. The same petite nurse with black hair walked in, followed by Kanoy.

Nina's bright disposition faded. All her self-talk was suddenly inconsequential. Kanoy had a way of casting doubt before speaking a word. She touched the crystal in her pocket.

"I need your fingerprints." Kanoy stepped forward, pleased with his announcement. Loudly chewing a wad of gum, he swallowed. "Someone's prints other than Sarah's were found on the syringe at the gallery." The chewing started up again.

Nina glanced at her father and then Kanoy. She clenched her fists to stop them from shaking. "Not here. Not in front of my father."

# THIRTY-EIGHT

Reluctantly, she gave her fingerprints to the police officer waiting outside her father's room. He reminded her of an art teacher she once had. Twitchy muscles causing jerky movements. Maybe not the best person for the job. It took two tries to land the print in the tiny box on the form.

Once home, she crawled into bed with a whiskey. A blush of ink remained on her index finger. She tried rubbing away the ink. The idea of going to bed dirty bugged her. Realizing the fingerprints reminded her of her father's in the book, she stopped. Happy with that thought, she set the untouched tumbler on the nightstand and turned off the light.

In the morning, she drove over to BrightStar. She had to make sure Kanoy's appearance hadn't riled her father. She walked in on *The Price Is Right* blaring on the TV. Nina turned it down before opening the curtains.

He looked the same. No eye movement. No crystal under the napkins. She filled his plastic water jug and dipped a straw into the child-size glass. With a heavy sigh, she sat beside him.

A thimble of Cream of Wheat consumed and two sips of orange juice later, Nina rekindled the people watching as strangers strolled by outside the window. A woman lugging a portfolio caught her attention. She wore a modest blouse, tailored black pants. Shoulders back, she had a fast-paced stride. Like the old Nina. She glanced down at her Broncos sweatshirt, wishing she were still that woman. Off to show her art, confident, driven toward something besides visiting Odilia. Today was the today. Despite the blue skies outside, the day felt fragile and she, unbalanced.

She shifted to her father. Saying goodbye was hard. She was glad he couldn't turn his head and see her tears. Head down, masking her tears, she hurried outside.

In the car, Nina was playing with the crystal when she called her mother. The call went to voice mail. Yesterday, Tisha had schlepped her wares to a gem fair. Nina examined the stone again. Had she seen this one before? She began scrolling through endless images on her phone. Too many looked the same. Even though she didn't believe in them, Nina was curious to know the meaning of this one. She considered telling the woman at the front desk about discovering the crystal. Maybe they would lock her father's door or post someone outside. If it wasn't Skylar, then who? She stared at the phone. *Mother, where are you?*

She called Jack after she had googled local gem fairs. Tisha didn't do overnighters anymore. Bad juju in hotel rooms, she said. Finally, something they could agree on.

Jack had an emergency patient and couldn't come with her to see Odilia, at least not right away. Nina's leg bounced nervously, listening to him. She wanted him there by her side when she confronted Odilia. Jack wholeheartedly agreed and refused to hang up until Nina consented to wait outside Odilia's house until he arrived. "Stay in the car. Don't get out under any circumstances. I'll be there as soon as I can." It had seemed silly at the time, but she had finally promised and set off to find her mother.

Black Forest, an unincorporated town thirty minutes east of Highway 25, proved not too far off the trek to Monument Lake where Odilia lived. Outside the hotel, the sight of the gem fair, a mammoth tent city sprawled the length of the parking lot. Nina followed the signs and parked in the gravel lot adjacent to the hubbub. She fingered the crystal in her pocket and hurried toward the maze of tents.

Inside, Nina blinked, adjusting to the dim light and heady smells. She scanned the open space. Tisha could be anywhere, sharing a table with a fellow mystic or tucked in a corner displaying her wares like the free-spirited gypsy she was.

Sun peeked in between tarps. The harsh light played tricks on Nina's eyes, making it hard to focus on the people. Incense mingled in the air, the potpourri of scents turning Nina's stomach. She traipsed past merchants, looking right, looking left. The baubles all looked the same: crystals, tarot cards, fragrant oils, books. Unique packaging and creative displays luring shoppers to step closer, peruse the mystical offerings.

A heady waft of burning sage tickled Nina's nose. She shifted, followed the smell. Often, her mother burned sage. As a child, Nina had enjoyed the woodsy, herbaceous funky aroma. One small part of Tisha's wizardry she had grown accustomed to.

Nina heard the lilt of her mother's voice. Who could miss the loud, Ms. Know-It-All, sarcasm-rich tone? She moved toward the spirited sales pitch she'd heard before. Sandwiched between two no doubt legit vendors, Nina found Tisha huddled at a card table.

"If it isn't my daughter," Tisha announced and pocketed the bills she'd just been given by a woman now drifting on to the next table. "I didn't expect to see you within ten miles of a gem fair."

Aware Tisha's booth buddies were watching, Nina smiled. "Nice to see you too, Mother." Motioning with her head, she signaled she needed a private moment.

Nina zigzagged and Tisha followed to the nearest glint of light poking in between a ripple in the tent. She pulled out the smooth, purple object and held it in her palm. "What type of stone is this?"

"Crystal," Tisha corrected, barely giving it a second glance. "It's a crystal. You should know that by now." She sighed. "No 'Hello, how are you?'" Her eyes playfully widened with mischief.

"This is serious. Please look at the st . . . crystal."

"I already looked at it. It's a chalcedony. One of my favorites." Tisha traced the striations. A twinkle danced in her eyes. "Sage goddess purple, they call it in the business."

Nina considered her words. *One of my favorites.* She pinned her mother with a steady stare. "Did you leave it in Dad's room?"

"Of course I did." She shrugged as if it were obvious. "You were distraught over your father's sudden outburst of anger at the mention of Odilia." Tisha rolled her eyes. "I never liked the woman, and—"

"Wait." Nine grasped her shoulder. "Stop, Mother. Just stop." She was struggling to stay calm, her mind flitting from one thought to another. A cymbal clanged, revving Nina's frustration to a ten. She sucked in a breath. If ever there was a time for a death stare . . . "Tell me everything."

Tisha wielded a simpering smile. It wasn't working. Arms crossed, Nina waited.

"You're not the only one who can visit your father," she started. "I was his wife, you know. Chalcedony brings comfort and calm. I thought your father could use the warm energy."

"That's kind of you. But you never mentioned you visited him." Nina tried to sound understanding. She looked at the crystal, realizing at this moment what bothered her more was something else her mother had said. "You knew Odilia?" Nina gulped.

"From a distance."

"Please, tell me you didn't know Sam Wood." Nina winced. The air seemed to thicken. A putrid whiff of incense burned her throat. "I need to know."

Tisha's eyelids flashed downward and away. "It was brief." She paused. "He had ambition. His life carefree, more or less. He was in a loveless marriage. No . . ."

"Children?" Nina said quietly.

Tisha nodded. "I wasn't ready for all of it." A weak smile betrayed her embarrassment. "For a time, your father had no clue. Always tucked inside a book. And his sudden painting interest." She rolled her eyes. "He didn't notice." She fiddled with the frilly scarf draped about her neck as if Cyrus's naivety validated her indiscretion. "Sam had asked me to meet him at the bookstore. I didn't know you were there." She was shaking her head in a convincing way. "Sam grabbed me. I twirled into him, around a corner into a cubby space of some sort." Tisha's eyes slid off Nina to the ground. "And there you were," she said in a small voice, trembling.

Nina couldn't form words. Disbelief clouded her eyes. Still, she locked on Tisha, ignoring the burn rising in her cheeks.

"Well, he kissed me," Tisha admitted.

Nina didn't know what she had expected. Shock? Anger? She refused to give her anything. "I was there? Watching you canoodle with another man?" Her words, ripe and smug, hung in the thick air. She had no memory of this.

"You were perched on a chair inside a room, like a crawl space beyond the postage-size room."

"The nook?" Nina hadn't noticed another room or a door. Only pillows and the colorful Eiffel Tower painting on the wall.

"I suppose that is one name for it." Tisha glanced beyond Nina. The edges of her lips lifted. "Propped on your knees in ragged overalls, you were painting." A tiny gasp, more like a giggle, escaped. "There was more paint on you than I imagine in that book. Or paper. I can't remember all the details." A jolt of surprise lit her face, then turned sour. "Your face. I do remember your face." Tisha dabbed the corner of her eyes with her scarf. "My little girl's mouth was gaping, terrified. Her brilliant-blue eyes had turned steel gray." She was talking in the third person as if Nina, the terrified little girl, wasn't standing right in front of her.

Tisha reached out to touch Nina, who stepped backward. She couldn't bear to look at her mother.

"After that, I called it off. It was too late. Your father had found out. And Sam was angry. Spat every word in the book at me and admitted he did something horrible to your father's painting."

"Why was I at the bookstore with him, Mother? Where was Dad? How could you two allow your daughter to be with him?" Nina cursed under her breath. She slanted away before snapping back, asking a question she'd never considered asking. "Did you kill Sam Wood?"

"I'm a healer. You know that."

"If that's what healing looks like, I want no part of it." Nina bolted toward the exit.

"Where are you going?" Tisha yelled.

"To see Odilia. Maybe she can explain to me what happened."

Tisha caught up to Nina and spun her around. Breathless, she clutched her arm. "Sam got over me in a heartbeat. But you . . ." Her eyes flitted about the space as if a tumble of images flashed behind her eyes. Finally, she locked on her daughter. "He kept asking about you. Even after he and Odilia had their own children. He showed up at your graduation. He was obsessed with you. Fascinated by your talent. Your art chops. That's what he called them. It irritated your father to no end. We asked him to leave you alone. Your father even threatened him."

"Did you ever tell the police?" Nina released her mother's hold on her.

Tisha shook her head.

———————

Nina's mind refused to unsee the vivid picture Tisha had described. *My little girl's mouth was gaping, terrified. Her brilliant-blue eyes had turned steel gray.* Turning off the highway toward Monument Lake, she couldn't settle down. Jack had texted. He was twentyish minutes away.

Years ago, Nina had painted at the lake. Part of a plein-air class with other artists honing their skills. Now, viewing the newer homes backed up to the lake with killer views of the foothills below Mount Herman brought little comfort. She coursed along the rolling hills on the lake's perimeter, tapping the steering wheel, finding anything to distract her. Knowing her mother knew Sam made seeing Odilia more crucial. The oxygen inside the car seemed to evaporate. Nina rolled down the window and sucked in fresh air.

Once close, Nina began hunting for Odilia's address. When she found the numbers on the mailbox, she pulled to the side of the road under a tree and parked. The brick house, somewhat secluded, sat a distance back in a stretch of flat land peppered with red oaks. Compared with Nina's condo, the house was huge, with shuttered windows and a wide porch. No one appeared to be home. No cars. No lights. Then again, it was daytime and there was a three-car garage.

It was quiet. Too quiet. A car whirred by, startling Nina. Then nothing for a good ten minutes. She alternated between glancing in the rearview mirror looking for Jack and staring at the house, wondering what Odilia was doing. Had she adjusted to life without Sam? And the children? How were they coping? If they were home, which seemed likely, Nina had to figure out a way to discreetly talk to Odilia alone. She could still picture them at the memorial tethered to their mother, awkward faces, trying to appear brave.

*Where is Jack?* She texted him. She'd been parked for half an hour when she heard the front door open. Odilia stepped out. Wearing cropped jeans and a blouse, she looked casual, almost approachable. Nothing like the severe updo and black business dress she had worn at the memorial. She walked to the spigot, turned on the water, and picked up a hose. Almost a postcard moment in the sun, shielding her eyes, an arch of water catching light.

Odilia shifted to the side yard and began sprinkling the shrubbery in a back-and-forth motion. Convinced she hadn't been spotted, Nina pulled out her phone and texted Jack again. *Where are you?* She stared at the phone, expecting an instant response. Then she scanned her emails.

Sensing movement, Nina glanced at the side mirror. Her heartbeat doubled. Odilia stood at the driver's side car window staring at Nina with a pencil-thin frown.

Nina gulped her surprise. Reluctantly, she rolled down the window. Slowly, her gaze rose to the woman.

"Out for a drive?" Odilia asked smugly, although she clearly knew that wasn't the case.

"I've come to see you." Nina forced an upbeat smile.

Odilia glanced up over the car, curled her lips in a weak smile. "It's a beautiful house, isn't it?"

Nina kept her eyes on her. "Picture perfect. You must love it here." She tucked her phone between her legs.

"I hadn't planned on visitors." Her eyes, wrinkled at the corners, darted side to side, thinking before trailing down to Nina. "I suppose I could show you Sam's studio. I assume you have questions about him, not me." She seemed to be put out and folded her arms, waiting. "I only have ten, fifteen minutes."

"Yes," Nina said carefully as if there was a catch. But she needed to wait for Jack. She looked down at the phone. Nothing. The rumble of tires passed by. Nina's eyes shifted to the vehicle.

"Are you expecting someone?"

Nina shook her head. *Stay in the car.* She'd promised, but Odilia's stern glare bore into her. Slowly, she slipped out of the car. Keenly aware of Jack's warning to wait, she maneuvered around the front of the car, never losing sight of Odilia.

———

Leaves crunched beneath Nina's feet. She followed Odilia along a dirt path. Not toward the front of the house. To a side entrance, less traveled. The path was overgrown, littered with weeds and soft soils. Forgotten.

While Odilia unlocked the door, Nina leaned back to glimpse the road partially obstructed by the house at that angle. A beat of nerves caught in her throat. A voice kept telling her to wait. To slow down, think things through.

Odilia cast the door open. Nina flinched at the squeak of worn hinges. "Not much use for the studio now." She waited a beat before following up the narrow, darkened stairs. The tight space smelled musty. And something else Nina recognized. A pungent pine smell: turpentine? She inhaled deeply and tried swallowing her concerns. *Every artist has turpentine,* she reminded herself.

The stairs opened to a bright, wood-paneled room with large windows allowing generous light to flood the space. "We built this over the garage when Sam sold his first commissioned piece."

Nina warily stepped inside the room. An easel sat by a window to catch the northern light. Windows flanked another wall. Painted canvases leaned haphazardly against walls. Polaroids and images ripped from magazines were taped to the paneling in various places: inspiration pieces. A handful of framed paintings hung too. Maybe his favorites.

"He spent most of his waking hours here." Odilia didn't look pleased and remained near the top of the stairs, arms crossed as if she was afraid to step farther inside. As if she would be breaching Sam's world.

Any artist would consider it a happy place, even inspirational. "I see why he liked it," Nina offered. The setup was an artist's dream. She slid a quick glance out the window. From the second story, she could see the hood of her car through the trees. No sign of Jack's vehicle.

"Not much more to see, really. All studios are the same, I imagine." Odilia turned to Nina, eyes wide, waiting for a question. At the same time, she looked perturbed. Her shoulder twitched as if being in the room spooked her. Odilia began tapping her foot, sending a faint echo into the silence. Her eyes narrowed on Nina who, at that moment, didn't speak. Odilia clearly was uncomfortable being in the studio. A sigh whooshed from her lips. She'd had enough and turned toward the stairs.

"Do you know anything about the art gallery in Crested Butte? Crescent Moon Gallery?" Nina blurted in one breath.

Odilia reached for the handrail, hesitating. Slowly, she turned to find Nina's brittle smile. "Oh, that," Odilia said matter-of-factly. She moved to a painting near the staircase and fussed with the frame as if it was off-kilter. "Not much to tell, really." She paused. "It had to do with you."

# 1985

# THIRTY-NINE

Cyrus glanced at the fire. The glow reflected upon his pale skin. Sam should have read the meaning of the silence. It was time to leave Cyrus and his home, but something kept him there.

"I should check on Nina."

When Cyrus flitted away, Sam drifted down the hall into the room where Cyrus had shown off *Paris Bench*. In the day, the easel had caught sunlight from the window. Unveiled, the layers of paint on *Paris Bench* glistened like the tips of churning waves. The phenomena, though interesting, didn't change Sam's view of the painting. Lifeless. Drab. He stepped closer, ran a thumb over the jagged slope of land, the layers of color no different than the sky.

He shifted to the palette beside the painting and studied the mounds of color. Without much thought, he grabbed a brush, dipped the tip in blue, and mixed it with the tiniest dab of purple. A palpable thrill danced in his chest. Poised inches from the painting, he hesitated. Before coming to his senses, he layered quick, feathery strokes on the canvas, defining the sky. Next, working feverishly, he mixed brown, black, and scarlet. The brush loaded with a volume of paint, he superimposed layers along the bottom of the bench. Next, the same hurried technique on the outward edges of the bench legs in shadow. Just a touch of color below the crescent underbelly of the tower. He glanced over his shoulder before blending another trio of colors and deepening the surrounding sky, propelling the Eiffel Tower to the foreground. Eyes wide and glowing, frenetic energy pulsed through his veins.

Sam heard footsteps. He put down the brush.

"What's going on?"

Sam turned.

For a beat, Cyrus remained at the doorway, his eyes traveling the room. He launched toward the painting. "Move aside," he ordered, motioning with a firm hand. "What have you done?" He gasped before a hand covered his mouth.

"Looks better, don't you think?" Sam believed that wholeheartedly. As much as he tried, he couldn't wipe away a smirk.

Cyrus's nostrils flared. "Who raised you to think you could desecrate another man's property? This is my painting. A gift to Nina." A deep inhale. "Leave this house immediately."

Sam's hands shot up. "Okay," he said, walking backward out of the room.

As he reached for the brass handle at the front door, he heard the squeal of a child and froze.

"You've finished." Excitement peppered the tiny voice, followed by a giggle. "It's the most beautiful painting I've ever seen."

No words fell from Cyrus's lips.

"When I grow up, I want to paint just like you, Daddy."

Sam couldn't help smiling. Little Nina loved his additions. He caught his reflection in the mirror beside the door. His right cheek slightly bulged because he'd thrust his tongue inside. Something his father did. Sam hated the look and considered it pompous, yet he was doing the same thing. A ceramic bowl sat on a table by the door. It caught his attention because of the handful of odd stones inside. Sam picked up a translucent one, admired the shiny thing before dropping it in his pocket. Everyone needed a lucky charm.

# FORTY

"You won his heart when you adored my husband's hand-iwork on *Paris Beach*. To think, the approval my husband had been waiting for came from a child," Odilia mused as she traveled to the next painting on the wall. She tilted her head, admired it as if she were seeing it for the first time. "He became obsessed with you. Cyrus's little darling. Nina this and Nina that," she groused. "'Nina can paint,' he'd say."

Facing Odilia's back, Nina didn't understand. "How did he know I could paint?"

*The bookstore.*

Odilia slowly turned and eyed Nina up and down. Nina felt the thick judgment. Part of her wanted to rush down the stairs, but she had to know. "How did he know I could paint, Odilia?"

Nina pinning her down, but Odilia wasn't a woman easily rattled. The arch of her brow, the slight tip of her chin upward said otherwise. She shed Nina's gaze and strolled to the table beside the easel.

"Why was I at the bookstore with him? Where was my father? How did I get there?"

"Sam took you on an outing," she said, almost upbeat.

"What do you mean?" Nina's heart began thumping.

Odilia picked up a random tube of color in a case and switched it with another tube like she was playing a game. "Sam passed by the house to see if your father was home. He was making book deliveries that day. You were in the yard flitting around, as children do. He thought it would be fun to take you to the bookstore to retrieve the book order from the nook and drop you back home before your father missed you." She looked brightly at Nina. "His intentions were well placed. A quick visit to the bookstore. No harm in that is there?"

"What happened in the nook, in that room?" Her mother had said enough to terrify Nina. But had something else happened? With Sam Wood? Something horrible? Terror stung like bees in her gut.

"Not what you think. My husband was a kind man," she assured her, but Nina wasn't convinced. Odilia's expression told a different story.

"Sam had discovered a secret door in the nook. The owner stored her prized book orders there. Collector books and whatnot. A storeroom, really, with a modest table, chairs, and a lamp. Sam offered you a gift. A book."

"What book?"

"Watercolor something something. I don't remember." Odilia shrugged, continued with her silly distraction with the paint tubes. "You flipped through the pages, asking Sam, 'What's this? What's that?' A whiny little girl bursting with interest, squealing over the painted pictures. How sweet." Odilia glanced at Nina, rolled her eyes. "Sam asked, 'Do you want to paint, Nina?'" Odilia twisted off the cap on one of the paint tubes and put it under her nose, like a perfume she was testing. "It was a kind gesture." She replaced the cap and turned to Nina. "Sam taught you how to paint properly."

The raw edges of an image formed, a tease near the surface, yet she couldn't quite see it.

*Oh my God.*

A breath caught in her throat. The vision came in a flash. The book. Glossy blue with bright-yellow letters. Thumbnail sketches on the pages showing her how to paint beside her awkward strokes, all the colors of the rainbow. *He* had called them practice strokes. "See if you can mix the exact same color," *he* had said. "See the light edging the cup." She had wrestled *his* hand away, dipped *his* finger in cerulean blue, and pressed *his* fingertip on the page.

*Sam Wood's fingerprint.*

A wave of disgust lodged in her chest.

She had reached for *his* hand, warm and clumsy. Not her father's slender and skilled hand. *"The book is yours to keep, a memory of how you learned to paint." He smiled. After they'd ducked through the door, back into the nook, he had handed her the book.*

Weeks ago, she had touched those faint-blue ridges. Nina rubbed her hands against her jeans, wiping away the memory. Eyes burning with anger, the room tilted. Or so it seemed. How had she gotten it wrong?

"Your father copied paintings from artists whose work was all but forgotten." Odilia stated matter-of-factly.

"No." Nina violently shook her head.

"It's true. Sam found a book at your house with a crude painting of the Eiffel Tower beside *Paris Bench*. Your father had no talent whatsoever."

Nina didn't believe it. She knew they had collaborated in the loosest sense of the word. But copying another painting? Nina closed her eyes. "What happened at Crescent Moon Gallery?"

"Your father agreed to show *Paris Bench* in a gallery outside of town."

"Broadmoor," Nina whispered.

Odilia shrugged. "Some Podunk town on the outskirts, away from people your father might know." She fingered another paint tube, skipped to the next. "He wasn't keen on the idea. Nevertheless, he agreed until . . ."

"What?"

"Sam slipped before the showing. Told your father about stealing you away. For such a calm man, I'd never seen someone's eyes bulge like your father's. He stumbled toward Sam, all for the gathering crowd to see. I suspected he might pummel Sam." She paused, held fast to Nina's eyes. One painted eyebrow arched. "As best as a man of his stature could muster. Instead, he nabbed the painting and stormed out."

The note in the book. Nina gulped.

*She's better than you, Cy. Talent skips a generation. Don't I know. Focus on her. SW*

From *him*.

Nina's eyes glazed over in disbelief. She looked at Odilia, vulnerable, like a child, desperate to know how the story ends. "After the bookstore he took me home?"

Odilia nodded. "You captured a part of him no one could. Even me. His wife. His biggest supporter. His listening ear, his dumping ground for all his doubts." A tremble had crept into her voice. "And all this." A frantic sweep of the room followed, eyes darting every which way. "It sickens me." With a backhand, the case of paints flew off the table, the wooden case splintering, the tubes scattering onto the floor.

Footsteps. Someone was coming up the stairs. *Jack?*

The little boy appeared. His eyes fell to the mess on the floor. "What is it, Andrew?"

Odilia's clipped words obviously hurt the boy, who looked up pale and listless. He lifted a hand across the shock of blond curls on his forehead. "My sugar's high, Mom."

"Be a good boy and go downstairs." She smiled coldly, waved a dismissive hand, wanting him gone.

With a bowed head, Andrew slowly turned and climbed down the stairs. When the door closed, Odilia sidestepped the jumble strewn across the floor and hurried to a cupboard. She tugged on the handles. "Don't presume it was only you." She poked her head out. "Alina, Claudia. Oh, and Bethany. All up and coming. Young and attractive artists."

Her eyes fell away from Nina to a red smear on her sleeve. A casualty from the paint splattering. She withdrew a rag from the cabinet. With rough strokes, she wiped the spot. "He thrived on attention. A selection committee chairman attracts women like you. But you were the last." She seemed delighted in that thought and sat with it a moment before continuing to scrub the stain with much more force than necessary.

Nina watched her smear the splotch onto her cuff. "There was nothing going on."

Odilia let out a huff. "You were having drinks. Don't patronize me. That's how it always started. An art contest, awards banquet, a gallery opening." She tossed the stained rag onto the table and rolled up her sleeve, her forearm now red and irritated. "I caught him once. I surprised him, showing up at one of his out-of-town judging obligations . . . " Her voice faded, and she glanced out the window. The light caught the side of her upturned nose, her thin lips held in a cultured, well-practiced downturn. She was hugging herself, lost in memories. For a moment, Nina felt sorry for Odilia, who seemed to have aged, sunk within herself, unable to carry the weight on her frame. Standing in the harsh light, the creased lines of her face deepened into a web of confusion.

"I didn't know your husband until the day I found him in the chair," Nina said gently.

Odilia came out of her reflective pause and primped with a bobby pin that had fallen loose as if a calm decorum had once again washed over her. She spun away from the window. "He kept a drawer with keepsakes. Pictures of you and others. Blurbs about your art, in particular. When he told me he'd nominated you for Best of Show, I was done." Her upper lip quivered. She raised a hand to cover her mouth. "You must leave now," she said calmly and began folding the soiled rag as if she were doing laundry. "You ruined everything." With quick steps, she carried the folded rag to the cupboard.

Andrew appeared again, this time carrying a small case. His face appeared blotchy, his breathing ragged. "My insulin, Mom. I need a shot now." He slid an insulin bottle from the case and held it in the palm of his hand before crumbling to the ground. The vial hit the floor with a clink and rolled to the middle of the room. The case spilled open beside poor Andrew.

A glint of sun caught the stainless-steel shaft of a hypodermic needle inside the case.

# FORTY-ONE

O dilia was looking at Nina. Not Andrew, collapsed and barely breathing. The needle in the case was no more than three feet away.

Nina tore her eyes from the needle to Odilia. A flash of fear flickered across Odilia's face. She stood frozen, kneading her hands.

Dawning, no doubt. The moment one realizes they've been made. *But her son?*

"Take care of Andrew," Nina said calmly.

Odilia didn't acknowledge she'd heard Nina. In fact, she wasn't even looking at Andrew.

Nina dropped to her knees, the wood beneath her creaking as she inched toward the case. She was close enough now to see Andrew's chest rise. His eyes fluttered open, his breath ragged. Relieved, she sucked in air before turning to Odilia, who was staring in another direction. "I've never given anyone a shot. You have to help me."

Nina had reached the case. She pulled out the needle and held it awkwardly. The vial of insulin rested in a shaft of light streaking across the wood floor where it had rolled after Andrew had dropped the case. Two steps and Odilia could easily pick it up. Instead, she moved to the cupboard.

Nina could hear her moving things on the shelf, but she couldn't see what Odilia was doing. She kept alternating glances between Odilia and the insulin. It would be quicker, she rationalized, if she crawled toward the insulin. Less motion to alert Odilia. She was almost there. Stretching out her arm, Nina snatched the bottle.

While she wrestled with the cap, she caught a glimpse of Andrew. Sweat glistened his brow. *"You're gonna be okay,"* she mouthed to him, followed by a brief smile. She made her way toward him and brushed a comforting hand over his damp hair. "Hang in there."

Nina knew what she needed to do next. She swallowed hard and picked up the syringe. A damned protective cap covered the tip of the needle. She yanked it off, poked the shaft into the vial, and pulled back on the plunger. She willed the syringe to fill faster. She had no idea how much insulin Andrew needed. Half? Full?

She looked up and gasped. Odilia was coming toward her, arm extended, holding a rag.

"Don't fight it," she said. "It was easy with Sam. Alcohol always put him to sleep. He didn't have a clue."

Sharp and vaporous, a putrid smell instantly burned Nina's nostrils. The rag she held was doused in turpentine, and Odilia was about to smother her with it.

There was no time to think. Should she slam the needle into Andrew's thigh (it seemed the obvious place) or get the hell away from Odilia?

# FORTY-TWO

ndrew wore jean shorts. Without care, Nina hiked up the denim and stabbed the needle into his thigh. Odilia was now above her, holding the rag over her nose and mouth. She was pressing hard, making it near impossible to breathe.

"Sam refused to poke Andrew with insulin. Always me doing everything."

Nina whipped her head from side to side, trying to unleash the rag.

"I showed him all right. How dare he ogle over you."

Nina tried holding her breath so the fumes couldn't enter her lungs. How long could she do that while clawing at Odilia, whose locked arms forced the rag to stay in place despite Nina's attempts?

"You, my dear, are the last floozy, his cherished protégé. You think you got your silly award on your own merit?"

A vile taste slid down Nina's throat. Strong vapors coated her mouth and her throat. Then came the burn. She tried to cough, but the effort was too much. Weak and dizzy, her head was pinned to the hardwood. All she could see was Odilia's distorted face: gray-toned but for a flush of pink on her fuzzy cheeks; squinted, moss-green eyes. Everything appeared shapeless. Nina fought as long as she could. Her eyes fluttered open. Odilia had morphed into a grainy, shifting shadow.

Everything grew quiet. Even Nina's breathing. Maybe she wasn't breathing. She struggled to open her eyes. She could feel tears pooling in the corner of them and streaming down her face.

She managed one more peek. One eyelid opened halfway. Another shadow appeared behind Odilia.

# FORTY-THREE

Nina scrambled to set up chairs. "Mother, six more along the wall. People from the news are coming." She bit her lip and glanced around the bare-bones space. Giddy and frantic at the same time, she hoped to God kids would show up from the residential home.

Nina swung around and caught Jack tossing brushes beside canvases like it was a race. "Jack, we have time. Take a breath." She found herself inhaling and breathing out slowly. He watched and mimicked her moves. Their eyes locked, and she felt his emotions bursting, same as hers.

Everyone had a task. Andrew and Alison buzzed around the room setting Styrofoam cups on the tables. Even Stacey had come to help.

Nina, realizing she needed a moment, stepped away from the chaos. Outside the building she'd leased two weeks ago, a banner hung cockeyed over the old signage. *Cam's House.* There hadn't been time to install the neon letters. Jack had a banner printed at Kinko's along with business cards. She'd finally gotten a business card with her name on it. Without the award listed, of course. That was still being decided.

Through the window, Nina spotted Jack, eyes wide, arms crossed, surveying the room. He was up on his toes, his craggy smile beaming like a proud papa.

The door swung open. Andrew popped his shaggy head out. "Can we come next week?"

"Of course." Nina tousled his hair. "You're a part of this thing, and so is your dad." No mention of Odilia. She was in custody without bail. The kids were staying with a distant relative in Fort Collins for the time being.

Nina had thought about inviting Stuart and his family. Turned out to be a coincidence that his family was staying at the Caspian ahead of their relocation to the area. She regretted jumping to judgment. Even more so, knowing Kanoy had hauled him in for questioning.

The bundle of nerves that had settled in Nina's stomach finally lifted. Maybe she just needed fresh air. And to see what she and Jack had created from a distance. Like with a painting, stepping back, you discern color balance, composition, and pattern. The mind then processes the piece as a whole. Only then can you fully appreciate what you've created.

Nina walked inside just as the projector flashed on. Tisha's photo filled the wall at the front of the room, A scenic view of Sedona. Brilliant orange hues, rugged rock formations, wispy clouds camping above. Her reasons for choosing it had to do with the supposed vortex in Sedona. Nina had simply liked the photo. She had photoshopped a superhero into the picture. Cam the Man. He's flying over a creek. Not the one in Jack's backyard but close enough. Jack hadn't seen the picture yet and was now staring at it, mesmerized. He swiped a hand across his eye.

Nina looked away and strolled to her work area at the front. As she walked, her fingertips grazed the tables where the children would paint, where she would teach. More like demoing a painting for the kids. Jack's idea. Instead of a paint-and-sip for adults, this was more of a slop-and-copy sort of thing with a few basic techniques tossed in. Of course, she had brought the book. It sat front and center beside her brushes.

Tisha shimmied up beside Nina. "Your father's coming with an aide," she whispered. "I wasn't supposed to tell you, but you know me." Flecks of mischief twinkled in her eyes.

Nina knew about the visit. The aide had called her to arrange the outing. It was his first. Of course, he would be the same frail man, but he'd be in a chair, they said, strapped and secure, watching his daughter in his own way. Nina touched her mother's arm. "Thanks." She pulled away and then remembered. "Oh, and thanks for the amethyst crystals for Dad. Helps with his speech. Good choice." She didn't get it and probably never would. Still, she refused to buy into the malarkey, but she had stopped rolling her eyes. The juju made her mother happy. That was enough.

"You're learning." Tisha winked.

"Kanoy would call it tampering." When he cuffed Odilia, he had looked defeated. Jack had happily called the jerk once he wrestled Odilia off me. Nina smiled at the thought. She had outsmarted him or at the least damaged his pride.

"Tsk." Tisha rolled her eyes. "That man needs prune juice." She scooted across the room.

Nina followed the sway of her mother's hips. She shook her head and smiled. Tisha brought life to any room. The opening wouldn't have been the same without her quirky style.

Alison's Mary Janes echoed on the tile floor, catching every-one's attention. She was chasing Andrew. "Come on!" she yelled. "Everyone is wearing an apron. Not just the girls."

"Why did you invite them?" Tisha asked Nina.

"Their father taught me to paint. Besides, I own a Cyrus Shubert/ Sam Wood original." Nina unfolded the apron on the table and looped it over her head. "He deserves that, Mother."

Tisha tossed on her own apron, less fussy about how it draped. She turned around, and Nina tied the strings.

Jack snuck up behind Nina and planted a kiss on her head. "What does he deserve?"

Tisha glanced at Nina, neither offering a word.

Jack looked concerned. "It's not about another fish, is it?"

# ACKNOWLEDGMENTS

B ooks are our babies. Birthing is hard, painful, and wonderful all at once. Thankfully, I have kind and thoughtful people who have helped me on my journey.

I have great adult children who are my biggest fans. Thank you, Britney Zint and Wes Barnes, for your cheerleading and advice from the beginning of my writing adventures. I want to be you guys when I grow up.

A bestie that always believes in you keeps you afloat. Wendy Reeves not only is *the* BFF, she is also *the* art aficionado. She inspires me and gets me. Splashing paint with her is the best.

I am indebted to Jill Linker and Denise Mitchell, whose support means the world to me. To Chrysteen Braun and Pam Sheppard, thank you for your insight and support.

Lastly and mostly, my banjo-playing husband, Dennis, who believed in me before we even existed. I love you morest. (I know. It's not a word, but it's our word.)

# BOOK CLUB QUESTIONS

Was Nina's fear that she may have done something to harm Sam Wood rooted in anything tangible?

Nina clearly believed she took after her father. What influence did her mother have on her in a positive or negative way?

Nina lived in the black and white, focused on one goal. What are some of the pitfalls in thinking this way?

Why do you think Nina couldn't paint after she became embroiled in the mystery?

Jack was Nina's champion, and she became his. Tragedy often divides. Why do you think that wasn't the case for them?

Nina idolized her father. How did that blind her from the truth about his painting and/or the book.

Do you think Nina's drinking and possible inebriation added to Nina's fears that she may have harmed Sam wood?

Has your focus ever been so narrow you couldn't see anything beyond your myopic view?

Tisha's beliefs were a stumbling block in her relationship with her daughter. Did you think Nina, or her mother handled their differing viewpoints properly?

Jack was wrestling with a serious issue. Did he leave the back door open when Cam fell at the creek? Was not knowing the truth a better alternative for Jack?

# *the* art *of* escape

### Book 2
### in The Galleries Series

### Coming 2024

Use the QR code or visit janmurphyauthor.com
for details on release date

www.ingramcontent.com/pod-product-compliance
Lightning Source LLC
Chambersburg PA
CBHW020142120726
47903CB00007B/2374